BATTLETECH:
ICONS OF WAR

BY CRAIG A. REED, JR.

BATTLETECH: ICONS OF WAR
By Craig A. Reed, Jr.
Cover art by Marco Pennacchietti
Design by Matt Heerdt & David Kerber

Published by Catalyst Game Labs,
an imprint of InMediaRes Productions, LLC
7108 S. Pheasant Ridge Drive • Spokane, WA 99224

Dedicated to officers and crew of the USS Gerald R. Ford: *may God keep you safe from any harm.*

Also to the late Jim Holloway, sci-fi and fantasy artist, whose early BattleTech *covers caught the attention of this twenty-something year old guy back in the mid-'80s. Thank you.*

ACKNOWLEDGMENTS

To John Helfers, who messaged me one day with, "You want a writing assignment?"

To Blaine Pardoe, whose idea this originally was, and who didn't mind when I came at this with a different angle.

To Philip Lee, who guided me from afar and kept me on target despite the rabbit hole I went down.

To Michael "Cray" Miller, who was a great help in keeping the last half of the book from violating too many laws of *BattleTech* physics, and the other fact checkers who helped smooth a few rough corners.

To my parents, who are still looking for that different drummer I march to.

To the *BattleTech* fans everywhere: you are the reason this game and universe has survived thirty-five-plus years. Let's make it another thirty-five.

CHAPTER 1

***BLACK LION*-CLASS WARSHIP CWS *STEALTHY KILL*
HIGH ORBIT, STRANA MECHTY
CLAN HOMEWORLDS
8 APRIL 3071**

Khan Vladimir Ward of Clan Wolf stood at the observation compartment's window, watching several DropShips and WarShips move across the face of Strana Mechty. If he had timed it right, the WarShip that would be the subject of this meeting would shortly come into view.

The hatch opened behind him. "My Khan?" a deep voice said.

Vlad raised his hand and waved the newcomer forward. He heard a couple of heavy footsteps and sensed the Star Commander's looming presence beside him. "A magnificent view, *quiaff*?"

"*Aff*," the Elemental replied, "but I was not called to Strana Mechty to admire the view."

Vlad looked up at him and smiled. "Your reputation for being direct is true, Garmen Kerensky."

Garmen's hair was short and dark, his face broad and flat, his eyes dark and full of intelligence. "We are both warriors, my Khan. You do not waste time with minor things."

Vlad nodded. "Very well, I will also be direct. I have a mission that requires someone of your talents."

Garmen cocked an eyebrow. "I am listening."

"First, what I am about to reveal is classified. I am only informing you to stress this mission's importance."

"I understand."

Vlad looked out the portal and took several seconds to order his thoughts. "Tamar was attacked with nuclear weapons in December. SaKhan Radick, most of the garrison, and millions of civilians are dead. The planet's industrial and administrative infrastructures are destroyed or heavily damaged."

Garmen tensed. "Who would do such a thing?"

"The Word of Blake."

"We should declare a Trial of Annihilation against them."

"I will not argue that." Vlad turned to the bigger man. "But we have other, more pressing matters to deal with. The genetic repository on Tamar was flooded with radiation from several warhead near-misses. The scientists—those still alive—estimate over ninety percent of the legacies are unusable."

"Great Father, help us," Garmen murmured.

Vlad raised an eyebrow in response. "In addition, the Hell's Horses have returned to the Inner Sphere in force, and have seized half a dozen worlds from us in the last several months. Both matters have made it clear to me the Wolves cannot remain divided, with one foot in the Inner Sphere and the other here. We are leaving the Clan worlds."

Garmen raised an eyebrow. "I see."

He turned back toward the window. "A top priority will be a supply of clean genetic material to rebuild our repository with. The best source of such material is down there, on Strana Mechty."

Garmen frowned. "Does that include Nicholas and Andery Kerensky's genetic legacies? It will be difficult enough to take the other Clan Wolf legacies from under the Grand Council's oversight, but the founder of the Clans and his brother?"

"They are Wolves, *quiaff*?"

"*Aff*. But the Grand Council will not see it that way. Many have tried to pry those legacies from us in the past. They will be furious if we take them beyond their reach."

Vlad snorted. "I am well aware of that. This is why I have been negotiating with other Clans for transport and warriors in exchange for our enclaves here and other concessions to prepare the way. But you are right about the Grand Council's reaction—removing our genetic legacies from Strana Mechty will provoke them into taking action against us." He looked at Garmen. "This is where you and your Star come in."

"My Khan?"

"We are in the final stages of preparing Operation Damocles, which will remove all of our genetic legacies from Strana Mechty. Damocles consists of three operations. The first operation, code-named Gladius, will remove all Wolf genetic legacies from the planet, except for the Kerensky legacies."

Garmen's frown deepened. "I do not understand."

Vlad smiled. "When the Grand Council discovers Gladius, they will likely declare a Trial of Abjuration against us. That we can handle—the Grand Council will not force the issue too strongly if the Kerensky legacies remain behind when we depart Clan Space. I want as much of our Clan beyond the Grand Council's reach before we reclaim our most important legacies. That is where you come in."

"Our task?"

"The second part of Damocles, code name Kopis, is the removal of the Kerensky legacies. That is where your Star is involved. Your role in Kopis will be as both extra security for the Kerensky Blood Chapel and monitoring the defending forces around Svoboda Zemylya. When we claim Nicholas and Andery's legacies, we will need up-to-date intelligence on defenses and the status of the genetic samples."

Garmen nodded. Svoboda Zemylya was a large park and nature preserve north of the capital, where the Hall of Khans and the Blood Chapels for each of the eight hundred warriors Nicholas Kerensky had deemed worthy of a Bloodname had been constructed. It was the political and spiritual center of the Clans, and there was always a strong military presence in and around it.

"What happens if the Grand Council claims the Kerensky legacies before we return to claim them?"

Vlad shook his head. "The Council is greedy, but they will wait until they are certain we are gone from Clan Space. I think a year, two years at most. We will be back to claim them before then."

He spoke into his perscomm. "Send Star Commander Niyol in." He looked at Garmen. "The Star Commander is unaware of what happened on Tamar. Keep it that way."

The hatch behind them opened, and another man stepped into the compartment. He was slightly shorter than Vlad, a little thinner, with reddish-blond hair and pale skin. "My Khan."

"Star Commander Garmen Kerensky, this is Star Commander Niyol of the Wolf Watch. He will command the Watch detachment assigned to you for Operation Kopis."

Niyol gave Garmen a nod. "Star Commander."

Vlad turned to face both warriors. "In addition to Kopis, there is a third part of Damocles—Operation Spatha." He looked out the window. "The *McKenna's Pride* is coming into view now."

Garmen saw the battleship. "I do not understand."

"I said we would not leave *any* Kerensky legacies behind."

"The Great Father?" Garmen asked, his voice barely above a whisper. He looked at his Khan, his expression one of shocked disbelief. "You want us to *steal* the Great Father's body?"

Vlad slowly shook his head. "I want you to *reclaim* the Great Father's body. When we remove Nicholas and Andery's legacies from the Grand Council's clutches, I do not want to tempt them into looking at the Great Father's remains as a possible replacement. If they want Kerensky genetic material, let them declare Trials of Possession against the Coyotes."

"What is our timetable?" Niyol asked.

"While Kopis is reclaiming the sons' legacies, the Grand Council's attention will be focused on that, allowing you to board the *McKenna's Pride*, reclaim the Great Father's body, and rendezvous with Kopis's JumpShip."

Garmen nodded. "We will need equipment and safehouses."

"The Watch will furnish some items, like false codexes, a couple of safehouses, and the location of a weapons cache, but anything else you will have to find yourself." Vlad stared at both of them. "I do not care what you do or how you do it as long as both Kopis and Spatha are completed."

"*Yes, my Khan*," the two said.

"Garmen, you are promoted to Star Captain, and are in command of Spatha."

"Yes, my Khan."

CHAPTER 2

Garmen stared at the assembled members of his Damocles team sitting in three rows of chairs in front of a blackboard. Twenty-four Elementals were dressed like Garmen in laborers' overalls. Niyol's Watch team was dressed in cheap suits common to low-level clerks.

They had gathered in a basement located in a laborer-caste housing complex, one of three Watch-provided safehouses. He had just finished giving an overview of Operations Gladius and Kopis, ending with, "We do not know when Kopis will happen—it could be weeks or months from now. You must maintain your cover identities at all times. Star Commander Niyol will pass out the assignments."

Niyol walked to the front of the group. "Your covers will be Blue Horizon Free Guild members hired to work as laborers at Svoboda Zemylya after the completion of Operation Gladius."

A few groans came from the Elementals. The Free Guilds held no allegiance to any one Clan, instead working for any of them, doing tasks the Clan had no people for. They were a necessary part of Clan society, though held in low regard by those within a Clan. That also meant Garmen's personnel would have to be tattooed with a tested-out symbol—a visible mark that they had failed as warriors.

Niyol glared at them for a few seconds then continued. "Three Points will be assigned to guard the Kerensky Blood Chapel. A fourth Point and my team will infiltrate the Hall of Khans and other locations in and around Svoboda Zemylya to gather intel on the military strength of each Clan's enclave. We will shift responsibilities and work shifts every two weeks. The command Point will act as a reserve while working on another operation, which the Star Captain will explain in a couple of minutes. Everything clear?"

Another round of muttered agreements followed.

Niyol nodded. "Now, assignments. Point Commander Adair?"

"Here." Adair was the Star's second-in-command. He was short for an Elemental, slightly over two meters tall, but broadly built, his heavy brow and wide jaw making him look more caveman than warrior.

"You will start as the infiltration team along with the Watch team. Point Commander Nokomis?"

"Here." Nokomis was pushing fifty but remained steady, reliable, and still succeeded in her yearly retests for warrior status. Her graying hair was cut close to her scalp, and there were wrinkles around her eyes.

"Morning shift at the Blood Chapel. Point Commander Ferko?"

"*Aff?*" Ferko was an ugly, scar-faced man known for his sour disposition.

"Afternoon shift. Point Commander Marsali?"

"Right here." The youngest Point Commander in the Star, her shaved head and eyebrows made her look like an ebony statue.

"Late-night shift."

Garmen stepped forward again. "When Gladius occurs in the next few days, it will enrage the Grand Council. They will be looking for any Wolves they can find, which is why you are posing as Free Guild. You *must* maintain your cover at all times and at any cost. The Chapel's senior Keeper and his second will know of your presence, but no one else will. A place inside the Chapel will be made for you to store weapons like rifles and grenades, so if it comes to a fight, you must fight as standard infantry."

After a few seconds of his warriors grumbling, Garmen continued. "I will not lie. It will be hard, but the Khan is counting on us. That means swallow your pride and focus on your mission. Understood?"

There was muttered agreement all around.

Garmen looked around the room. "While our Clan reclaims Nicholas and Andery's legacies, we will be executing Operation Spatha."

He walked over to the blackboard and turned it over, where a ship's deck plans had been taped. Several seconds of silence followed as the warriors' puzzled out the implications.

"This is Spatha," Garmen said, eyeing his warriors. "Khan Ward has decided that in addition to the genetic legacies of Aleksandr Kerensky's sons, we are also taking the Great Father himself back with us."

That drew a few shocked glances among the warriors, along with a few murmurs of surprise and disbelief, while others frowned in puzzlement.

Garmen continued. "Using the chaos that is bound to happen during Operation Kopis, we will board the *McKenna's Pride*, seize the Great Father's body, and rendezvous with a Wolf JumpShip that will carry us back to the Inner Sphere."

The room became silent for several seconds as the mission's goal sank in. Garmen let the silence draw out before continuing. "The infiltration team will gather intelligence on the *Pride*'s security measures. My Point will be working on gathering additional resources and intelligence."

Garmen's eyes swept the room once more. "Point Commanders, make sure your warriors train regularly and meet once a week for operational planning. Any questions?"

There were none. "All right, Niyol will give you each a new codex, a month and a half's worth of work credits, and your assigned quarters in Svoboda Zemylya. A tattoo machine in the next room will mark you as failed warriors—it is a temporary tattoo that needs to be redone every three weeks, so you must schedule a time to refresh it. I want your new identities to be second nature before we move in. Dismissed."

"I am opposed to dealing with the Dark Caste," Niyol said once the others had collected their new IDs and left. Besides them, only Garmen's aide, Wymer, remained.

Garmen removed the deck plans from the blackboard. "You know we have limited resources. We need transport to the

Pride, knowledge of the *Pride*'s security, and more equipment. We also need funds and contacts, and the best way to get all of that is to deal with the Dark Caste."

Niyol shook his head. "Just remember that you cannot trust those *stravags*."

Garmen snorted. "I do not need to trust them to utilize them."

"Understood." Niyol gathered his notes. "I will speak with you tomorrow."

After Niyol left, Garmen looked at Wymer while he folded the plans. "You have stayed silent."

The freebirth Elemental was larger than any of the Point Commanders, his face scarred, his hair short and white. He was the oldest warrior in the Star, with decades of service, and Garmen often used him as a sounding board. "The only question I have is who came up with this insane plan?"

Garmen shook his head. "The Khan orders and we obey." He picked up the deck plans. "Help me clean up, then we can get some sleep."

CHAPTER 3

Old Katyusha was the parts of the original Katyusha City that had survived Nicholas Kerensky's new capital being built on top of it. Wedged between the five quarters of the new city, the five sectors of the old city—northeast, northwest, south, southeast and southwest—housed the Free Guilds and a few low-ranking Clan members.

Garmen and his Point used the city's elevated monorail system to travel to the sector's edge, then walked the rest of the way. All five wore Free Guild laborer clothing, but each was armed with a pistol, and Wymer and two others had shotguns concealed under their coats. Both foot- and vehicle traffic was light, but they did see the several pairs of patrolling, white-uniformed Katyusha Keshik troopers, the city's police force.

The bar was between a food store and an eatery. It had a large sign over the door reading simon's. Inside, the air was smoky and bitter, the patrons rough-looking, and Garmen felt the hostile stares directed at him and his team when they walked in. Wymer and the others returned glares of their own, promising sudden violence at any provocation. The hostility lessened, but it hung in the background like a coiled cloud cobra.

Wymer and Garmen headed for the bar. The bartender, a short man with a shaved head and cold gray eyes, watched them approach. "Whadda you want?"

"Two Viper's Tears and some black bread," Garmen replied. The code phrase registered in the bartender's eyes. "Bread'll be a few minutes." He pulled two bottles from under the counter and placed them on the bar. "Four work credits."

Garmen placed a small, cloudy-blue topaz on the counter next to the bottles.

The bartender palmed the gem and leaned close to Garmen. "The empty table in the corner."

Garmen and Wymer grabbed their beers, walked to the table, and sat down with their backs to the walls. The rest of the Point—Gada, Dewi, and Zevin—scattered to different parts of the barroom. Wymer popped the bottle top off with his thumb and took a long pull. "Tastes more like Viper's Piss," he muttered, putting the bottle down.

"Be nice," Garmen said, opening his own bottle.

"I always am."

The last three months had been an eye-opening trip through Katyusha City's underbelly. The riots stemming from Operation Gladius had led to a week-long, dusk-to-dawn curfew throughout the city. Once the curfew had been lifted, Garmen and his Point headed to the weapons cache.

Located several hours outside of Katyusha City, the cache contained a full Trinary of second-line 'Mechs and an infantry Cluster's worth of weapons and equipment. Garmen immediately dismissed the 'Mechs as useless to him.

On the other hand, the small arms were the perfect entry into the Dark Caste. They had transported most of the weapons to an Old Katyusha safehouse, then using Niyol's Dark Caste contacts, Garmen had sold them small batches of weapons, earning a small fortune in gems, which were portable, retained value, and couldn't be tracked. They'd quickly established themselves as a prime source of weapons and gained a reputation for being ruthless against thieves who tried stealing a weapons shipment.

Today's meeting was another step deeper into the Dark Caste. A buyer interested in a large weapons deal had contacted Garmen. They had named the bar as the meeting place, and the time was now.

After five minutes, the bartender brought over a plate of black bread and left without speaking. Another five minutes passed before a lean man with short dark hair appeared from a door next to the bar. He strolled over with a languid stride, but Garmen saw the alertness and wariness in his expression.

"This seat taken?" he asked in a low voice, motioning to a chair.

"*Neg*," Garmen replied, placing his bottle on the table.

The man sat. "I'm Balbas. I hear you have good merchandise."

Garmen frowned. The use of contractions among the lower castes still rankled him. "Depends. What are you looking for?"

Balbas smiled, making him look boyish. "Forty rods, a hundred eggs, two stovepipes with a dozen birds each."

Forty rifles, a hundred grenades, two mortars, and a dozen rounds for each mortar. Garmen nodded. "That is doable."

"My boss is willing to make a deal. Shall we continue this in her office?"

Garmen shifted into alertness. "Of course."

Balbas rose to his feet. "Follow me."

Garmen glanced at the rest of the Point, made a "stay put" gesture, then he and Wymer followed Balbas to a hallway with a staircase. Garmen noticed several security cameras in the hallway and two more covering the stairs. "My boss is upstairs."

"Who is your boss?" Garmen asked warily.

"She is known as the *Zimnyaya Ledi*—the Winter Lady."

Garmen frowned. "I have heard rumors that she always wears a mask, and no one knows who she is."

"That's right. She's interested in meeting you."

Garmen glanced at Wymer, made a hand gesture to stay alert, then followed Balbas up the stairs, his hand staying close to his pistol.

At the top of the stairs, a single glowstrip illuminated a short, featureless hallway with a door at the far end. Balbas knocked on the door before opening it.

The office was like every other office Garmen had been in—function over style. It had a desk facing the door, a pair of chairs, several file cabinets, and several pictures on the wall. There was a bank of monitors on the wall to his right, showing images of the bar, the hallways, the stairs, and both the front and back doors.

The woman leaning against the desk with her arms folded dominated the office. She was Elemental tall, but lean and trim instead of bulky like most Elementals. Her hair was long and platinum blond, framing a white mask with smooth, feminine features and red eyes. She wore a skirt that went below her knees and a blouse with the top two buttons undone to show cleavage. "You are the arms dealers?" she asked in an electronically altered voice.

"*Aff*," Garmen replied. A nudge in the back of his mind said this woman was familiar.

"I am the *Zimnyaya Ledi*. Can you supply our needs?"

"I believe so."

"If you can, there might be a more permanent arrangement down the road."

Garmen's mind continued nudging, telling him this Winter Lady was familiar. "I see."

"Do you?" There was mirth in the woman's voice. "Tell me, Garmen Kerensky, what is a Wolf Clan Star Commander really doing here on Strana Mechty?"

Garmen froze, but Wymer stood, his shotgun coming up.

The woman held up a hand. "No need for a fight, Warrior. The Star Commander and I are old comrades." Slowly, the *Zimnyaya Ledi* removed the mask, revealing a beautiful face with sparkling blue eyes that Garmen remembered at once. Her smile was predatory. "Been a long time, *sibkin*."

He stared at her, not believing who she was. He opened his mouth to say her name, but her laugh cut him off.

"Call me Satinka," she said. She looked at Balbas, who stared from her to Garmen in puzzlement. "I know this man. Go keep an eye on the others while we talk."

"Right, Boss." He stepped out and closed the door behind him.

She motioned toward the closed door. "Balbas is my right-hand man. Come, sit down. I'm always happy to see a *sibmate*, especially you, Gar. What are you calling yourself these days?"

"Yama."

"You're looking good." Satinka put the mask on the desk and walked over to a sideboard, where she added ice to three glasses. "Your friend can lose the shotgun."

Wymer made his weapon disappear back under his coat. "You two know each other?"

"Of course," she replied, pouring liquor into the glasses. "We were in the same *sibko*. I just go by a different name now." She picked up two glasses, walked over to the two men, and offered one to each.

Garmen took the glass. "It has been awhile."

"Fifteen years. Sit." She walked back over the sideboard and picked up the third glass. Then she sat down behind the desk, leaned back, and looked at him. "Now, Gar, why are you really here?"

Garmen sipped the liquor. It was strong, leaving a pleasant burn behind when it went down. "I am here making deals. I have weapons, you have money."

"You're avoiding my questions."

"I have my reasons."

"I know you, *sibkin*. And you are still avoiding my question."

"I am here to negotiate a deal."

Satinka smirked. "All right, we'll play it your way. Let's talk."

CHAPTER 4

Bhu Telinov knocked on Star Colonel Gavril Mikino's office door and waited for a gruff "Enter" before opening the door and walking in.

She walked to the front of the desk and came to attention. "Star Captain Bhu Telinov reporting, sir."

The Elemental sitting at the desk looked up and glared at her. "Welcome to the Ebon Keshik," he said in a deep voice, his tone cold and hard. He had a face full of hard lines and angles, and his short hair was cut close to his scalp. He looked foreboding in his black uniform and dark expression.

"Thank you, sir." Telinov was the Star Colonel's physical opposite. She was slim, with short dark hair and blue-green eyes, and her own black uniform was razor-sharp.

"I will be blunt, Star Captain. I do not like the idea of non-Elementals in the Ebon Keshik. But the ilKhan and the Grand Council have decided that the Keshik's Watch detachment needs *new* blood." He let the stressed word hang in the air between them, half insult and half challenge.

Telinov felt a flash of anger. It was not her fault the Ebon Keshik's Watch had failed to discover the Wolves' plan to retrieve their genetic legacies in April until it was too late to stop it. Nor was it her choice to be here, after the entire Keshik Watch had been removed and replaced with new personnel—

most of whom were *not* Elementals. "May I speak bluntly, Star Colonel?"

"You would be a poor Watch commander if you did not."

Telinov kept her expression impassive. "I have been assured by my Khan that the personnel assigned to this task will only be here for a couple of years. The Watch's failure to detect the Wolves' removal of their legacies made the Grand Council look for scalps—including your predecessor."

Mikino's expression darkened, but he nodded. "You will be taking over as the Keshik's Watch commander from Star Captain Horan Baba, who proved...difficult to work with. I hope we will not have the same difficulties, *quiaff*?"

"*Aff*, sir. I do not think so."

"Good. Your deputy is Star Commander Sergis Steiner. He will bring you up to speed."

They went over a series of details, mostly about her responsibilities and what to expect as a member of the Ebon Keshik. "You may think of this as a temporary posting," Mikino said in conclusion, "but the Ebon Keshik takes our responsibilities seriously. Until your Clan reclaims you, the Ebon Keshik *is* your Clan. Your job will be handling intelligence matters that affect *all* Clans. You will hold nothing back, even things that may help your own Clan. The Ebon Keshik serves as the Grand Council and the ilKhan's eyes and ears. We handle problems that threaten our society before they can rise to the Grand Council's attention. Always remember that, and your time here will be a credit to your codex. Dismissed."

Telinov knocked on the office door of her new deputy commander and waited for a reply before entering.

The office was smaller than Mikino's, and not as clean. The man who rose from behind the desk was above middle height, lean, with dark hair and an angular face. "Star Captain!" he said with a grin on his face.

"Star Commander," she said with a smile, and strode over to the desk. "I like what you have done with the place."

"It is homely."

"It has been, what, three years?" She sat in one of the chairs in front of his desk. "Any problems with me taking command?"

"*Neg*." He sat down himself. "It is good to see you again, Bhu."

"You too, Sergis."

"Did the Star Colonel give you the glare and the talk?"

Telinov nodded. "He is unhappy that non-Elementals like us are in his Keshik."

"That is putting it mildly. He and Star Captain Baba clashed repeatedly over minor items. That is why you are here and he is not. Now, where to start?" He waved at the papers on his desk. "We are looking into a dozen different matters right now, and you need to get up to speed on them. You also need to meet the analysts and get an idea of their strengths." He thought for a moment. "I know how we can do both, but not before we get plenty of coffee ready."

After the ninth analyst left the Ebon Keshik's conference room, Telinov slumped into her seat. "Great Father," she moaned. "How many more are there? I am dying here!"

Next to her, Steiner chuckled. "Told you coffee was important. The good news is only one analyst is left, but I warn you, Kyne is in his own Cloister, so to speak."

Telinov arched an eyebrow, but said nothing as Steiner called for the next analyst. The warrior who entered was slightly above medium height, thin, with a plain, forgettable face. His green eyes focused on Steiner first, then Telinov. He stared at the military awards she had pinned to her new black uniform.

"Star Captain," he said softly. "MechWarrior, Josian Cloister, Remembrance Bar, Cross of Devotion, Ninety-Seventh Cobra Guard, Beta Galaxy, Clan Cloud Cobra." He came to attention. "Star Captain Bhu Telinov, I am Warrior Kyne."

Telinov looked at Steiner, who spread his hands. "I said nothing. Kyne did the same thing when I arrived. He has a photographic memory, an eye for detail, and an ability to take data from a dozen different sources and create a coherent report from them. Star Captain Baba used him for complex, long-term projects."

Telinov nodded then looked at Kyne. "What is your current project?"

Kyne's voice was a monotone. "Analysis of Bandit Caste activity in several systems around Homer. Over the past three years, Clans Cloud Cobra and Star Adder have suffered nineteen percent increases of ship and cargo losses in that sector of Clan Space. I have narrowed the bandits' base to one of three systems, and have compiled an estimate in the size and composition of their force."

"I see." Telinov leaned forward. "How much longer do you need for your analysis?"

"Less than a week, Star Captain."

She nodded. "What is your next project?"

"Just my default project, which is detailing and tracking the Dark Caste gangs here in the city."

Steiner smiled. "Who is the most elusive Dark Caste leader here in Katyusha City?"

"That would be the *Zimnyaya Ledi.*"

Telinov frowned. "Who?"

"Give us the overview," Steiner said.

"*Aff*, sir. May I use the holographic interface?"

"Go ahead."

Kyne moved to a panel on the conference table and began tapping buttons. A hologram appeared above the table and began to rotate slowly. It was a white mask with feminine features and eyeholes.

"The first confirmed appearance of the *Zimnyaya Ledi*—Russian for the Winter Lady—was six years ago," Kyne began, "in the company of the *Zimniy Korol*—the Winter King—the notorious smuggler and leader of the *Snezhnyye Siroty*—Winter Orphans. She is described as being as tall as an Elemental, but we cannot be sure of the source. The *Zimniy Korol* vanished six years ago, either because he is dead or has retired, and the *Zimnyaya Ledi* assumed control."

"No way to identify this person?" Telinov asked.

The analyst gestured to the hologram. "*Neg.* She wears a mask like this one when doing business, and uses a voice modulator to disguise her voice."

"Base of operations?"

"We think somewhere in Old Katyusha's southern sectors."

"Threat level?"

"Unknown. It is impossible to find reliable data."

"That is enough," Steiner said with a smile. "Finish up your current assignment, and I will see if there is another case you can work on."

"*Aff*, Star Commander."

"Dismissed."

Kyne snapped to attention, spun, and marched out of the room.

When the door closed, Steiner leaned back. "Do not let his demeanor fool you, Bhu. Kyne is up for the next Banacek Bloodname, sponsored by the commander of the Adders' Alpha Galaxy himself. You give him an assignment and enough time and data, he will tell you what the person had for breakfast two weeks before."

"What was with the briefing on this—"

"*Zimnyaya Ledi*? She operates one of a dozen Dark Caste groups inside the city. Tracking them is the closest thing Kyne has to a hobby."

"I see." She yawned. "What time is it?"

"Past noon. Have you seen your quarters yet?"

"*Neg*. I do not even know where they are."

"I will show you. Come on."

CHAPTER 5

The table in the small eatery's back room held the remains of a large meal. Garmen wiped his mouth with a napkin and looked at Satinka, who leaned forward and smiled at him. "Now will you tell me why you're here?"

"To sell weapons," Garmen replied.

"I still don't believe you."

He leaned back. "Why do you care?"

"I like puzzles, and you're an enigma."

"Why are you using contractions? You were not raised that way."

She laughed. "I'm Dark Caste now. We speak however we like, and to hell with traditions."

Garmen looked at her. The *sibkin* he had known fifteen years ago had changed. She had always been slim for an Elemental, but she had been as fast and tough as any of their *sibmates*. She had been the closest to him, and they had found chemistry both on and off the training field. When paired together, they worked as a team, each one anticipating the other's actions as if linked to the same mind. That closeness skirted the training regulations, and it caused them to be assigned to different Points for their Trials of Position. Garmen had won his; she had not, and he was unwilling to ask why.

"Gar, what's on your mind?"

He was startled out of his thoughts. "What?"

Satinka smiled. "It may be fifteen years since we've seen each other, but I still know you better than anyone else. I can see the questions in your eyes, but you're not sure you want the answers."

He nodded. "You are right."

She leaned back in the chair and looked at him like a cat watching a mouse. "What do you want to know first?"

He looked down at the table. "I—"

She snorted. "We've been dancing around each other for the last month! Every time we meet, you talk business and shy away from anything personal. But I know you too damn well, Gar. You want to ask, but you're scared of the answers. Ask away. You won't hurt my feelings."

He sighed. "Your Trial of Position—what happened?"

"What do you know?"

"Nothing. You were gone, and I was on my way to my assignment a day after the Trial and never found out."

"I see." She inhaled. "The trial was a disaster from the start. First, all our missiles went haywire and missed. Then, our suits' radios went dead and we couldn't coordinate. Finally, my suit's myomers froze up and I could barely move. Our opponents hammered on me until the armor failed and I was knocked unconscious. When I came to, all the radios and what was left of my suit were working again, like nothing had happened."

He frowned. "That is suspicious."

"Of course it is!" she snarled. "I was sabotaged! Oh, I appealed, and they went over the suits and found nothing. With no evidence, my appeal was rejected, and the trial's results were upheld. End of story."

"Who do you think was behind it?"

"Laya. She had the technical knowledge to sabotage the suits, and she was jealous of our friendship. I saw her once, six months later, and by the smirk on her face, I knew she had done it."

"For all the good it did her. She was crushed by a Hell's Horses *Warhawk* six years ago."

Satinka laughed. "A fitting death for a *surat*."

"What happened after that?"

She became somber. "I tested down to the merchant caste and was apprenticed to a man named Jarlath. He was a good mentor, and he taught me well. We were on Bearclaw seven years ago, when a merchant we were negotiating with decided Jarlath's price was too high, so she had him killed and tried intimidating me into selling the merchandise at her stated price—JumpShip, DropShip, and all. 'Why steal the egg when you can take the chicken?' she said to me and then smirked, just like Laya did!"

Garmen grimaced. "That was a bad idea."

"It was. I'll admit I lost my temper and killed the *stravag* and both her bodyguards, but I was quickly identified and had to run. Fortunately, one of Jarlath's friends, Zorian, was a Red Willows Free Guild DropShip captain who dabbled in smuggling, and I paid him to smuggle me off Bearclaw. What I didn't know was Zorian was both the Red Willows Guildmaster and the infamous *Zimniy Korol*—the Winter King—leader of the *Snezhnyye Siroty* and the most wanted smuggler in Clan Space. The Red Willows is the *Snezhnyye Siroty's* legal front."

She closed her eyes. "Zorian took me under his wing and taught me everything about both the legal and illegal sides of the guild. I became his protégé and took the name *Zimnyaya Ledi*. When Zorian died, I became the new Guildmaster and leader of the Winter Orphans."

"You became Dark Caste."

She laughed and opened her eyes. "You make me sound like I should be in a cave in the wilds, wearing furs and hunting for my food!" The smile faded. "If it hadn't been for Zorian, I might have ended up doing just that. But while some Dark Caste live outside Clan society, some prefer living inside Clan society, hidden in plain sight. We're both *chalcas*, just in different ways."

She leaned forward again, her smile hungry. "Enough about me. How about dessert?"

Garmen woke slowly, head pounding and mouth dry. He opened his eyes, grimaced at the bright light filling the room, and closed them again. He sat up slowly, only to wince from an explosion of pain behind his eyes. "Freebirth!"

"Good morning."

He cracked his eyes open, wincing at the brightness until his sight adjusted. Satinka sat in a chair, fully dressed, watching him. He then realized he was naked, in bed. "What happened?"

"We drank, came here, and coupled." She tilted her head and smiled. "Despite being drunk, you were amazing." She stood, picked up two pills and a glass of water, and handed them to him. "Here."

He swallowed the pills and chased them with the water. "Thank you."

"You're welcome." She returned to her chair and stared at him for a long moment, a small smile forming as she leaned back. "I have ears and eyes everywhere, Gar, and they have told me some interesting things about you."

"Such as?"

"Around the same time you appeared, there was an influx of new hires, most of them Elementals, up at Svoboda Zemylya. They're registered with the Blue Horizon Free Guild, but I know Blue Horizon doesn't employ that many Elementals. Also, some of us Guildmasters suspected Blue Horizon of being a Wolf Watch operation."

Garmen groaned. "Make your point already."

Her smile became predatory. "Most of the new hires are working at the Kerensky Blood Chapel—five on each shift. Another ten have been working in and around the Hall of Khans."

Garmen's head was beginning to clear, and the pounding began to recede "So?"

"So these new workers at the Blood Chapel are armed—they're carrying pistols, and rifles and heavier weapons are hidden inside the chapel. There have also been several hacks into the Hall's computer systems when Blue Horizon members are working."

"You should be a storyteller," Garmen growled.

Satinka sighed and held up the pouch containing the *McKenna's Pride*'s deck plans. "What about this? My people found it hidden in your safe house."

Garmen threw the covers off and got up, only to stop at Satinka's hungry gaze looking him up and down. "I was in a hurry last night," she said, "but what I see now is *very* nice. You have really filled out."

Snarling, Garmen yanked the sheet from the bed and wrapped it around himself. He did not know why he was angry—nudity was common in *sibkos*, and they had seen each other naked more than once, but her look made him uncomfortable. "It is not your business!"

"I'm *making* it my business," she replied in an amused tone. "It's obvious you're here gathering intelligence and protecting the Kerensky legacies."

"You are—"

"Don't think because I'm no longer a warrior that I'm an idiot, Gar. Sooner or later, the Wolves *will* be back for the Kerenskys' genetic legacies." She stalked over to him until they were close enough to touch. "We both carry Andery Kerensky's DNA, and the Kerensky legacies belong to the Wolves, not the Grand Council." She held up the deck plans. "And the only thing on the *McKenna's Pride* worth the Wolves' attention is the Great Father himself."

Garmen tensed up. "What do you want?"

"I can help you. The Winter Orphans have ears and eyes everywhere and a long reach. I can get you whatever you need. Equipment, people—name it, and it is yours."

Garmen felt torn between kissing her and strangling her. "In return for what?"

The predatory smile was back as her arms slinked around his neck. "You, for as long as I can."

CHAPTER 6

SOUTHEAST SECTOR
OLD KATYUSHA
STRANA MECHTY
CLAN HOMEWORLDS
2 DECEMBER 3071

They lay together in the bed, covered in sweat and a single bedsheet, Satinka's head on Garmen's chest. They lounged there, listening to the silence.

The apartment was a *Snezhnyye Siroty* safehouse. As the Red Willows Guildmaster, Satinka had an office in the Central Sector's Free Guild Hall and a mid-level apartment in the Merchant Quarter. But as the *Zimnyaya Ledi*, she had several safehouses scatted across the city. They never used her official apartment, nor did Garmen visit her Free Guild office. Instead, they did business at the bar's office and conducted "discussions" at one of the safehouses.

The last three and a half months had been a whirlwind. The rest of the Star continued their duties at the Kerensky Blood Chapel, but over Niyol's objections, Garmen had withdrawn the infiltration team from the Hall of Khans. Satinka had successfully argued that her people were in better positions to gather the necessary intelligence without revealing themselves.

The Watch officer complained until the flow of data from Satinka's sources trickled in, dwarfing the amount of data the infiltration team had gathered—enough to keep his team busy sifting through it. It had taken Niyol two months to grudgingly admit the data was better than what the infiltration team had gathered. They now had a full breakdown of all units currently stationed at Svoboda Zemylya and dossiers on most of the high-level commanders. The intelligence on the *McKenna's Pride* was less plentiful, but they had enough to plan the assault.

In addition to the intelligence, the *Snezhnyye Siroty* had located a *Gazelle*-class DropShip for transporting the strike team to the battleship, and a shell guild was used as a front to buy the ancient vessel. They had spent two months making the newly christened *Botany Bay* spaceworthy and recruiting members of the guild to man the DropShip. Once repaired and staffed, the *Botany Bay* had performed several cargo runs for the Red Willows, to test both crew and vessel. Other supplies and equipment for the assault were gathered through the gang's network of contacts.

The last of the preparations for Spatha happened two weeks ago. Now it came down to the waiting.

"Gar, what's the Inner Sphere like?"

He looked down at her. "What do you mean?"

She looked up at him, her expression melancholy. "Is it paradise?"

His relationship with Satinka had been both a bane and an asset to the mission. Their relationship from fifteen years ago was just the starting point, and had become even deeper and stronger over the last four months. He was not ready to call it love, because he had no reference. He was a Clan warrior; emotions such as love were for the lower castes. At the same time, it felt right to him, *she* felt right to him, and as hard as he tried, he could not shake the sad thought of leaving her behind.

At the back of his mind, he knew this was wrong, that this relationship would not—could not—last. Once Spatha was executed, he and his warriors would be leaving Clan Space forever. His mission came before anything else, his orders clear and from the Khan himself.

He ran a hand across her face. "That is not a simple question."

"Why not?"

"There are thousands of planets and I have only seen a handful, mostly in combat."

"All right, what are the worlds you've been on like?"

"Like here. Some planets are harsh, unyielding rocks that are a struggle to survive on, while others are more hospitable, and some are amazing. Why do you ask?"

She closed her eyes. "I wish I could see them."

The innocent words cut deep into his heart. Before he could answer, his perscomm buzzed on the nightstand. Frowning, he sat up and picked it up just as Satinka's own perscomm buzzed. "Yes?"

"Kopis is green," Niyol said.

Garmen threw off the sheet and rose. "Understood. Time?"

"Twenty-four hours. Data sent."

"Alert the Star. Spatha is green."

"Understood. Out."

He turned to Satinka, who was already on her feet, her resigned expression telling him everything. "It's starting."

"*Aff.*"

"My contacts say half a dozen DropShips are coming in from the zenith point, using Clan Coyote transponders."

"Niyol says the intelligence has been sent."

"Then this is goodbye."

"*Aff.*" He was silent for a moment. "Thank you for your help."

"Do what you need to, Star Captain. Follow your orders." He could feel her bitterness, and winced at another stab of regret.

He dressed quickly, not looking at her. When he was done, he turned toward her. "Be well."

"You too."

He left, knowing she would not cry until he was gone.

CHAPTER 7

From the safehouse's second floor, Garmen saw fires burning across the city. To the north, thick, dark smoke hung over Svoboda Zemylya as fierce battle raged around the Blood Chapels.

Garmen wanted to be in that maelstrom, the call to battle singing in his veins. But his battle was on the *McKenna's Pride*, the Great Father's body his priority.

Wymer came up behind him. "We are ready."

Garmen turned. He wished he was wearing Elemental armor, but he was still dressed for war in an olive-drab field uniform and flak armor. "DropShip ready?"

"*Aff.* Marsali says everything is still quiet at the DropPort at the moment."

"Good. Let us go."

The plan was simple: they would drive to the laborer DropPort, board their ancient *Gazelle*-Class ship, and using the recognition codes acquired by Satinka's people, dock with the *Pride*. They would move swiftly to overwhelm the guards, disable the ship, and reclaim the Great Father's body. Once the body was aboard the *Botany Bay,* they would head to the waiting JumpShip.

The plan lasted all of five minutes after they left the safehouse.

The fighting had spread beyond Svoboda Zemylya, beyond the Warrior Quarter and into Katyusha City itself. Fights were everywhere as mobs fought mobs, attacking anyone not of their Clan. Both of Garmen's trucks were targeted by rocks, bottles, and other debris. Twice, their caravan drove through improvised roadblocks, and both trucks suffered cracked windshields.

Six blocks from the DropPort, Garmen's radio crackled. "Five to Six!" Marsali voice was hard to hear over the static. Her Point was already at the DropPort, guarding the *Botany Bay.*

"Six here," Garmen said.

"The SCC has grounded all nonmilitary craft!"

Anger slashed through Garmen. The Space Control Center monitored all intersystem space traffic. "Keep the crew preparing the ship."

"But—"

"We are fifteen minutes away. Any other problems?"

"Several large fights have broken out within sight."

"Protect the *Botany Bay* at all costs, Five."

"Copy. Five out."

A more substantial roadblock appeared in front of them. The few civilians manning it fled when Garmen's warriors jumped out of the trucks and charged. His team quickly pushed the vehicles aside to let the trucks through.

Two blocks later, a massive street fight with dozens of civilians blocked their route. Garmen scowled and ordered both trucks to back up and try the next street over.

They found rubble blocking the next street, forcing them to back up and try another approach. Garmen noted several specks in the distance, either birds or aircraft, but he was too focused to pay any attention to them. "Six to Five, status. We are having problems reaching the DropPort."

"Copy. A mob just rushed another DropShip near us. Looks like they are trying to board it."

"Understood. Get inside the *Botany Bay* and seal it until we arrive." The specks were getting larger, moving toward him from the south at a high rate of speed.

Aerospace fighters.

"Copy, Six. We are moving inside the DropShip and sealing it."

Garmen saw the aerospace fighters losing altitude in a manner that suggested a deliberate act. "Be advised, Five. Aerofighters coming in from the south. They may be making an attack run near your location."

"Copy, Six, we see—"

The fighters opened fire at a ground target. It was only then he realized the target was the DropPort itself. Several large explosions, black smoke and orange fire rose above the buildings between the strike team and their destination.

"Five!" Garmen yelled into his radio. "Answer me! Marsali!" He looked at Zevin, who was driving. "Get us there now!"

It took them another hour to reach the DropPort, but one look at the flaming wreckage of the facility was enough to tell Garmen they needed a new plan. Four DropShips, including *Botany Bay*, were burning. Aerospace fighters still flew overhead, fighting each other or striking targets on the ground.

The air was heavy with smoke and sickening smells. Garmen's team searched for *Botany Bay* survivors, but found none.

"What do we do now?" Wymer asked.

Garmen looked at his warriors. "We retreat and reassess."

CHAPTER 8

Smoke still hung heavily over the city when Garmen and his Point returned.

While reports indicated mass destruction around Svoboda Zemylya, the damage in Katyusha City was worse. Entire city blocks were either destroyed or heavily damaged, and thousands of people dead. Public transport had shut down, and too many streets were blocked by rubble or too damaged to allow vehicular traffic. A few shops remained open, but the power grid was heavily damaged. A thick layer of gray dust covered everything, and the smells of death and destruction reminded Garmen of the battlefield. No one paid his Point any attention as citizens cleared away rubble, while others checked damaged buildings, everyone wrapped up in their own grief and shock.

"Madness," Wymer muttered, and Garmen silently agreed.

After leaving the DropPort, Garmen and his team had gone to the weapons cache and stayed there while the fighting continued. Later that day, he watched an orbital bombardment strike the city, erasing an entire block in a blink of an eye. The cache's military radio indicated fierce fighting raged everywhere.

Garmen's first urge was to go into the city and find Satinka, but he shoved that thought aside, as both his warriors and mission took priority. But worry and unease gnawed at him until after ten days he could stand it no longer. He had to find out if she was all right. Wymer and the rest of his Point had insisted on coming along to "assess the damage."

It was late in the day when they reached the bar and the neighborhood around it. The area had suffered some damage but otherwise was quiet and intact. Inside the bar, a few patrons sat hunched over their drinks with an air of heavy despair clinging to them.

Balbas stood behind the bar, looking tired, his clothes appearing slept in. He nodded at them. "You survived."

"I lost people. How is she?"

"Upstairs, piecing together what's left of the guild and the *Snezhnyye Siroty*."

Garmen nodded. "I am going up." He looked back at Wymer. "I will not be long."

Wymer shook his head. "She will never let you out of her sight again." He ignored his commander's glare and said to Balbas, "What is the best beer left?"

"Iron Monkey. Four bottles left, ten work credits each."

Wymer nodded, took out a ruby, and placed it on the bar top. "Give me all four, keep the change."

Garmen left them and went up to Satinka's office. He was about to knock when the door flew open, and someone grabbed him by the collar and yanked him inside. He flew across the room and slammed into the desk hard enough to crack the wooden front.

As he rolled onto his back and sat up, the door slammed shut. When his eyes finally focused, he saw Satinka standing between him and the door, hands on her hips, her expression unreadable. She looked tired and disheveled, but there was a gleam in her eye.

"Hello," he said, feeling like an idiot.

Satinka dove at him, landed on top of him, and grabbed his head in her hands as she kissed him hard. She broke the kiss and hissed, "Talk later."

She kissed him again, and neither one said anything for a while.

Garmen ignored Wymer's raised eyebrow when Satinka and he walked into the barroom two hours later. She looked at Balbas, "Any Huntress Dark Amber left?"

He glanced under the bar. "Half a bottle."

"Bring it and four glasses over to the corner table. We have business to discuss."

Balbas cocked an eyebrow, then nodded and reached under the bar.

Wymer looked at Garmen. "You did not talk upstairs?"

Garmen felt a flush of embarrassment heat his cheeks. "It is...complicated."

"Ah." Wymer rose from the table where the rest of the Point was sitting, and followed Satinka and Garmen to the corner table. Balbas carried a liquor bottle and four glasses to the table and sat down.

Satinka filled each glass and passed them around. "You are still here. What happened?"

"I lost five and the *Botany Bay* when the DropPort was strafed. You?"

"Three dozen guild members and twice as many *Snezhnyye Siroty* confirmed dead. Most of our warehouses were destroyed, and most of the guild's revenue is gone. Other gangs and guilds were also hard hit, and several were destroyed outright."

"The city?"

"The official death toll is fifty thousand and climbing. Out at Svoboda Zemylya, the Ghost Bear, Snow Raven, Jade Falcon, and Star Adder enclaves were destroyed. The city services are overwhelmed, and the hyperpulse-generator station was destroyed by fire. Reports indicate the Wolves blew up both the Kerensky and Winson Blood Chapels, and the genetic samples of both Kerenskys and Jennifer Winson were stolen from the Master Repository."

Garmen felt relief flow through his team. "They did it," he said softly.

Satinka sipped her liquor. "They did. Destroyed half the city and turned the entire Svoboda Zemylya into a war zone in the process, but they did it."

"There is a lot of chaos out there," Wymer said.

Balbas sipped his drink and smiled. "Chaos is also opportunity. We should take advantage of it."

Satinka nodded slowly, her expression thoughtful. "Agreed. You've been pushing me for years about turning the *Snezhnyye Siroty* into the major Dark Caste player in the city. I think it's time." She looked at Garmen. "You still wish to carry out your mission, *quiaff?*"

"*Aff.* Though I do not know how to do it."

"You'll need a base of operations, continuing intelligence access, and equipment, including a JumpShip. I can't do any of that right now, but if we take advantage of the chaos, we can build an organization that can supply everything you need and more."

"In return for what?"

"An alliance. We've a chance to take control of the city's Dark Caste, but we need people who can fight. Your people."

"It will take you months or even years to consolidate power."

"It's going to take time to assemble the resources you need. If you help us, you can get what you need faster with less risk."

"She is right," Wymer said.

Garmen exhaled quietly. Part of him wanted to argue, but they both were correct. "All right. What is our first move?"

CHAPTER 9

Standing behind and to Satinka's right, Garmen watched two of the *Tenevyye Nozhi*—Shadow Knives—carry a hooded and cuffed man to a steel chair in the circle of light. One of them removed the captive's hood before stepping back into the darkness.

The prisoner, a middle-aged man with a balding pate and a long face, winced and put up his hands to shield his eyes from the light. "Who are you?" he said in a quavering voice. "What's this about?"

"Senior Technician Acis," Satinka said. Her tone was cold, her affected accent further modified by her mask's voice modulator. "You are a poor gambler and a former Wolf collaborator."

The prisoner tried peeking around his hands to see her, but Satinka stayed beyond the circle of light. "Who are you?"

She stepped forward just enough so her white mask caught the light. "Who do you think?"

The man froze and his eyes went wide. "No! The *Zimnyaya Ledi* is not real!"

"What's real is your debt to me. You owe me sixty thousand work credits."

The technician's expression shifted from disbelief into panic.

Over the last four years, the *Snezhnyye Siroty* and their leader had become *the* power in the city's Dark Caste. Three weeks after the meeting at the bar following the destruction of the DropPort, they controlled the entire southeast sector of Old Katyusha. A month later, most of the gangs in both the Merchant and Scientist Quarters had been theirs. Now, the *Zimnyaya Ledi* controlled 80 percent of the illegal activities in the city and had become an urban legend.

Satinka's merchant experience allowed her make deals that benefitted everyone, but there were times when Garmen's warriors had to handle things. But as the organization grew, it became clear that they needed more enforcers to impose the Winter Lady's will. Reluctantly, Garmen agreed to organize and train the newly created *Tenevyye Nozhi* in return for picking the cream of the recruits for Operation Spatha II. Now, with a force of two hundred trained and armed enforcers, Garmen's warriors were reserved for important actions and the continual training of more Shadow Knives.

"I can pay it back!" Acis shouted.

"That will take years," Satinka replied, walking around the circle of light, forcing Acis to follow her voice. "But you can work off your debt. You are the senior Free Guild DropShip maintenance technician at the Laborer Quarter DropPort, *quiaff*?"

"*Aff*, but—" His eyes went wide. "No drug smuggling! The Ebon Keshik would execute me if I get caught!"

"Calm yourself, Acis," Satinka replied, sounding amused. "I would not waste you on smuggling drugs or contraband. I have another task in mind for you."

Garmen, wearing a suit and a steel mask, carried a case into the circle of light. He placed the case in front of the technician and stepped back into the darkness.

"There are two dozen recording devices inside," Satinka said, still walking around Acis, letting the light briefly catch her mask. "You will splice one device into the computer system of each and every DropShip that comes through your maintenance bays. Or would you prefer talking to the Ebon Keshik about your previous work for the Wolves?"

"Y-y-you can't prove I am a spy!"

"I have proof, and I am sure the Hammers and Fists would like to see it."

Acis went even paler at the nicknames for the Ebon and Katyusha Keshiks. "Why are you doing this to me?"

"Simple. This so-called Society has been bad for business, both here and elsewhere. The—"

"I am not one of those Society *stravags*!"

"I never said you were. The Society is a bunch of fools trying to upset the balance under the delusion of equality. They will fail in the end. But they are hurting our business, and the failure of our normal communication methods is becoming intolerable. These devices will give us a better idea of conditions in Clan Space. You have the skills and access to install these into the DropShips' systems, and if done right, they are undetectable."

"W-what is to stop me from going to the Hammers and Fists and spilling my guts?"

Satinka laughed, the voice modulator making it sound mocking and sinister. "I am the *Zimnyaya Ledi,* an urban legend—you said so yourself. And the devices will not help your story—they are easily built from common, untraceable parts. In the end, they would simply fire you for even attempting to tell such a crazy story."

Acis deflated. "I'll do it, but will you keep your word?"

She stepped into the light just enough for him to see the smooth, feminine, pure-white, mask with red eyes. "I do keep my word. As an incentive, for every device you install, your debt to me will be reduced by five hundred work credits. Fail to do this task, and you will *regret* our next meeting." She stepped back into the darkness. "Give him the case, show him how to get more, then get him out of here."

Garmen stood in a corner of the warehouse's office, while Wymer sat on a couch, both without their masks. They watched Niyol pace the office, his now-gaunt face looking pensive.

"I hate this," the Star Commander muttered.

"You wanted intelligence, didn't you?" Satinka said, her mask and wig lying on her desk. "We cannot plan in a vacuum. Our offworld sources are either dead or not responding, and several of our JumpShips and DropShips are missing. Normal interstellar transportation is in shambles, so I cannot send people out to look. The devices are not perfect, but they will allow us to get an idea about what's going on and plan accordingly."

Niyol continued pacing. "We have become Bandit Caste. We are falling away from the warrior's path and becoming criminals."

Satinka shook her head. "We can't move now anyway. WarShips are moving in and out of this system, and several are always in orbit. The SCC is on high alert in case someone tries to invade the system. Any assault on the *McKenna's Pride* would be impossible."

Niyol stopped and glared at her, then walked out of the office.

After a few seconds, Satinka said, "Someone's on edge."

"He is unhappy that we are taking civilians with us," Wymer said.

Satinka looked at Garmen. "I thought that matter was settled."

"It is, as far as I am concerned. Niyol is annoyed that I did not consult him before agreeing."

Satinka folded her arms. "I'm not changing my mind. I'm coming with you—me and anyone else from the guild who wants to come along. That's nonnegotiable."

"And I agreed. As far as I am concerned, the matter is settled."

"Niyol needs to relax," Wymer said.

Satinka smiled. "He's in luck, because I know just the right woman for the job. I'll call her later."

CHAPTER 10

"We have the first data recordings from the devices Acis planted," Niyol announced, "and it's worse than we thought."

The *Snezhnyye Siroty* and Spatha II leadership held full meetings once a week, at different places and times. Satinka, Garmen, his Point Commanders, Niyol, Wymer, and Balbas sat around a table in a private room in a closed eatery. They were all dressed in laborer, merchant, or technician garb, and all looked tired. Outside, two of Garmen's Points and two squads of *Tenevyye Nozhi* guarded the building.

Niyol looked down at his notes. "The good news is most of the fighting in Clan Space has ended, but the data indicates there was a lot of bloodshed. As far as we can determine, the Fire Mandrills and the Ice Hellions are no more."

"Not going to lose any sleep over them," Adair growled. The other Wolves nodded and muttered agreement.

Niyol also nodded. "The data also indicates that the Society had taken control of a number of worlds and either killed the population or used them as test subjects in twisted experiments. The few solid reports we have are unsettling, to put it mildly, as are the reports of plagues sweeping through several planetary populations."

The reaction to this announcement was less blasé. Garmen noticed unease among his Point Commanders. Satinka frowned in thought, but Balbas's expression remained cold and stiff.

"Does that make our mission easier or harder to execute?" Wymer asked.

"Our mission is on hold until we can overcome several obstacles," Garmen said. "This war with this Society is only one of them."

Niyol nodded. "The Khans are still using the *McKenna's Pride* as a meeting hall while the Hall of Khans is undergoing repairs. Security is still heavy—intel indicates there is still an Ebon Keshik Elemental Trinary and two aerofighter Stars on board."

"Freebirth!" Adair growled. "How much longer can it take to repair the damage caused by a single out-of-control aerospace fighter crashing into it?"

"One that did enough damage to threaten the Hall's structural stability. The Ebon Keshik is taking no chances on poor construction."

"Any estimate on the repairs being completed?" Garmen asked.

"Best guess right now is the end of the year."

"That's two months longer than the last estimate!" Ferko snarled.

"It's not my fault!" Niyol shouted back, his face reddening in anger. "I'm not in charge of the reconstruction!"

Garmen narrowed his eyes. His warriors' speech was becoming courser over time—contractions and more Dark Caste manner of speech were infiltrating their language. Niyol was right: they were slipping from the warrior caste into the Dark Caste. Time to remind them they were still warriors.

"Enough!" he barked as he stood. "I know we are all on edge. Niyol is right; we cannot affect the speed of the hall's repairs. Until the Grand Council decides to move their meetings back to the Hall of Khans, there is nothing we can do except prepare and be ready to move when our opportunity appears. But we have other problems—the Space Control Center for one."

He looked at each one of his warriors. "We made the mistake of not taking the SCC into account the first time, and Marsali and her Point paid the price. I had not realized how much authority the SCC has regarding the system traffic and defense until after our attempt failed. Until we find a way to neutralize the SCC, we cannot execute Spatha II."

"I hope you aren't suggesting we send the *Tenevyye Nozhi* to hit the SCC," Balbas said.

Garmen shook his head. "That building is a fortress. We would need an Elemental Trinary to even make the attempt."

"You have 'Mechs. Why not use them?"

"Because the only three MechWarriors we have are part of my Watch team," Niyol replied. "The Katyusha Keshik headquarters is only two blocks away from the SCC, and they will quickly react with overwhelming force, no matter which direction we come from. We would be cut down before we can even get close to the Central Sector."

"And Niyol and his team will be needed on the *Pride*," Garmen finished.

"Assuming you had pilots for those 'Mechs," Satinka said, her head cocked and a smile on the corners of her mouth, "could they destroy the SCC before the Hammer and Fists stop them?"

"It would be a suicide mission, but *aff*, they could." Garmen's eyes narrowed. "What do you have in mind?"

"Not what, but who. I won't say anything more right now."

Garmen exhaled and sat down. "Fine. What about the JumpShip?"

"We're in the process of acquiring what's left of the Gray Lotus Free Guild. They've a *Star Lord*-class JumpShip that's perfect for our needs—it has a lithium-fusion battery and had an overhaul just before the Society reared their heads. We're refitting several DropShips to carry cargo, people, and a place of honor for the Great Father."

"How long?"

"I don't want to rush things—that will attract attention. We're forming a new guild and placing all the Spatha JumpShips and DropShips into it, then we'll funnel supplies and people who want to come with us to this new guild. Six to nine months is a safe time period."

"How about the Spatha personnel?"

"I have a list of technicians. They all have JumpShip experience, and several have WarShip experience. When we finalize the team, I'll assign them to one of the new guild JumpShips and keep them away from Strana Mechty until we're ready."

Garmen nodded. "This has been a long road, longer than we expected, but we are getting close. We cannot start making mistakes now. Point Commanders, we will start rotating your Points every two weeks instead of every month—two weeks at the cache, two weeks in the city as Red Willows Guild members and *Tenevyye Nozhi* enforcers. All Spatha training will be at the cache. We will clear out a few storerooms to use for training purposes."

He looked around the table. "Point Commanders, time to discuss your warriors. Adair, we will start with yours."

CHAPTER 11

NORTHWEST SECTOR
OLD KATYUSHA
STRANA MECHTY
CLAN HOMEWORLDS
9 AUGUST 3075

The bar was two blocks from the Technician Quarter, in an area filled with housing complexes. Night had fallen, and the rain poured steadily, making Garmen appreciate his rain poncho. Next to him in the alley, Satinka waited in her own poncho, looking amused. Wymer stood a few meters farther into the alley.

"Why are we out here and not in the bar?" Garmen growled.

"Him," she replied with a motion of her chin to a man striding toward the bar. Garmen didn't see much more than a lined face and steel-gray hair around the cap he wore before the man disappeared inside the bar.

"Name is Stas," she said. "A Wolf Trueborn warrior who was a *ristar* thirty years ago, but ended up a Smoke Jaguar bondsman just before Operation Revival."

"He never regained his warrior status?"

She snorted. "Not with those arrogant *surats*. After the Jaguars' destruction, he joined a Free Guild, but most of his guildmates were killed during the Wolves' attack on the Kerensky Blood Chapel—an orbital strike destroyed the guild's shelter. Now, he works for any guild that needs extra hands. That's why we had a hard time finding him."

"Will he talk to us?"

"We can but hope."

Garmen turned to Wymer. "We are going in. Alert Nokomis to maintain the perimeter."

"Understood."

Garmen and Satinka crossed the street and went into the bar. The place was full of low-and medium-level technician caste, and none of the patrons were of Elemental stature. As soon as they entered, everyone stopped and looked at them.

A trio of muscular techs rose from their chairs to confront them. "What're you doing here, strangers?" asked a woman with old burn scars across her face.

"Looking for someone," Satinka replied.

"This someone have a name?"

"Let 'em through, Ardala," a voice said from a corner both in the back. "They're here for me."

Ardala frowned. "You sure, Stas?"

"I'm still sober, so yes."

Ardala scowled and stepped aside. "Careful of your step, *Bulk*," she snarled, using a derogatory term for an Elemental. "Start something here, and we will finish it."

Garmen nodded and walked past her. Satinka followed.

Stas was sitting by himself in a booth, a beer in front of him. Garmen judged the man's age to be twice his own, with sharp, hard eyes. "Soon as I saw you two in the alley, I figured you were here for me." Behind them, the bar noise rose as the customers went back to drinking and talking.

Satinka slid into the booth and struggled to get comfortable. "You're a hard man to find."

"I don't move around much." He looked from Satinka to Garmen. "What do you want?"

"They say you're Trueborn," Satinka said.

He glared at her. "I stay away from politics." He sipped his beer and sat back. "Have for thirty years."

"You're just planning to sit here and slowly drink yourself to death?"

"Unless you're here to offer me the glory of a warrior's death, then yes."

"And if we could offer you such a thing?" Garmen asked.

Stas shot him a cold look. "That's not funny."

"I am not joking."

Satinka folded her hands in front of her. "After the second Wolf raid, you said the Grand Council was, and I quote, 'fools with no regard for human life.'"

He looked back at her, his face dark with angry. "I was furious. One of those WarShips—I don't know which one—destroyed a building filled with civilians, including Bela, my partner for twenty-five years. The Grand Council struts around and act as warriors, but thousands died because the Wolves came back to reclaim what was theirs, and Grand Council reacted like spoiled children!"

He took a long pull of his beer. "If you've come to arrest me, do it. If you've come to kill me, do it. I don't care."

Garmen looked around, noticing a few glances in their direction. He crouched next to the booth so he was at eye level with Stas. "There are a few Wolves still here, roaming the wilds—a few ghost wolves looking for one last hunt."

Satinka placed a card on the table in front of Stas. "Call us if you want in."

They stood and walked away. Near the door, Garmen looked back and saw Stas looking at the card. Then the former warrior looked up and stared in their direction, his expression unreadable.

Wymer met them outside. It was still raining, and only a few people were on the street.

They had walked two blocks from the bar when Garmen's perscomm beeped. He stopped and answered. "Yes?"

"This a single person job, or a team?" Stas asked.

"A team."

"In the city, or outside?"

"Outside to start with, but it will end up in the city."

"Length?"

"Unknown at the moment."

"Are you supplying the equipment?"

"We are. It might need some work to make it operational."

"I see." Stas was silent for a few seconds. "Assuming I take you up on this offer, can I bring an advance team along to discuss more of the details?"

"As long as it is not too large."

"No more than three other people. Give me a week to get in touch with them. Good?"

"That is fine."

"All right, count me in. I'll contact you later. Good night."

Once the conversation was over, Garmen broke the connection and sighed.

Satinka asked him, "What's wrong?"

"Four years ago, I would never have had a conversation that obscure."

She laughed. "In a couple of more years, you'll be using contractions like the rest of us."

He shuddered. "I hope not."

CHAPTER 12

CENTRAL SECTOR
KATYUSHA CITY
STRANA MECHTY
CLAN HOMEWORLDS
14 AUGUST 3075

The knock at Bhu Telinov's office door made her look up from her paperwork. "Come in."

The door opened, and Star Commander Sergis Steiner stepped inside. "Busy, Star Captain?"

"Not really."

He smiled and closed the door behind him. As both were Cloud Cobra MechWarriors, and two of the few non-Elementals assigned to the Ebon Keshik, they shared a comradeship—a necessity in the whirling storm of the last six months.

The victory over the Society had revealed deep wounds among the still-remaining Clans, and the Society's lingering influence still managed to poison those wounds. First, Clans Ghost Bear, Jade Falcon, Snow Raven, and Diamond Shark—the rest of the Inner Sphere Clans—joined the Wolves in Abjuration, their assets in Clan Space forfeited, and all their Bloodnamed warriors subject to Reaving upon contact.

Then, the Goliath Scorpions had to defend themselves against claims they had absorbed an Inner Sphere mercenary unit, and only the Scorpions presenting reasonable evidence that the mercenaries were all dead kept the incident from becoming another Trial of Abjuration. Surprisingly, Kyne had noted in the report that this incident had the potential to become a problem later on.

Clan Coyote, the primary source of the Society rebellion, felt the Grand Council's anger. The surviving Coyote warriors were each subjected to a Trial of Cleansing—a modified Trial of Refusal—while the Clan's entire scientist caste was subjected to a Trial of Annihilation. The aftermath left the Coyotes without a scientist caste and a severely weakened warrior caste. If Telinov had her choice, she would have declared a Trial of Annihilation on the entire Clan and destroyed them all with orbital bombardment, but ilKhan Brett Andrews had decided to be generous. Also on the losing end of a Trial of Refusal, the Hell's Horses forces that remained in Clan Space were reborn as Clan Stone Lion.

But things had taken an ugly turn a few days ago. During a debate over delaying the entire Clan eugenics program due to uncertainty about the purity of the remaining genetic legacies, Star Adder Khan Stanislov N'Buta called for a Trial of Reaving against Clan Steel Viper. IlKhan Brett Andrews, a Steel Viper, declared a Trial of Refusal, then killed N'Buta with a laser pistol, only to die minutes later when the Adders' saKhan, Hannibal Banacek, beat Andrews to death with his own Viper mask. The result was the declaration of a Trial of Annihilation against the Steel Vipers and Hannibal Banacek being elected as ilKhan. The Viper warriors assigned to the Ebon Keshik had vanished overnight, leaving holes in the command structure. Telinov had been appointed the Ebon Keshik's deputy commander, and Steiner was appointed Watch commander.

She noticed he was holding a pair of folders. "Problem?"

Steiner smiled. "Quite the opposite. Kyne did it again."

She raised an eyebrow. "What?"

"He thinks he has identified two members of the *Snezhnyye Siroty*'s inner circle."

"Really?" Telinov sat back in her chair. "I thought he was working on the Viper *touman* estimates."

Kyne had turned out to be the best analyst Telinov had. He had predicted the Wolves' return to reclaim the Kerensky legacies—why the report was not acted on still mystified her—and he had uncovered the Society's propaganda and recruitment cells on Strana Mechty by digging through hundreds of reports and connecting dots no one else saw. Without his efforts, Telinov did not think the Ebon Keshik could have broken the Society's on-planet network as quickly and completely as they did.

He nodded and handed her one of the folders. "The Viper *touman* estimates."

She laid the folder on the desk. "I will make sure the Grand Council gets this before the day is out. The *Snezhnyye Siroty*'s inner circle?"

He gave her the second folder. "Here."

She opened it and looked at a couple of photos. "Who am I looking at?"

"Guildmaster Satinka, of the Red Willows Free Guild. Her background is a bit fuzzy, but Kyne thinks she is Dark Caste, maybe even be the Winter Lady herself."

"Any proof?"

Well, in the last four years, while most other guilds suffered, she managed to not only keep her guild above water, despite heavy losses, she bought out two smaller guilds and came out ahead."

"She is a good merchant, nothing wrong with that."

Steiner motioned with his hand. "Check the next page. It lists her payments and expenses over the last four years. See anything odd?"

Telinov scanned the page until she reached the bottom. "Her expenses exceed her income."

"By nearly twenty million kerenskys."

"Satinka is not in debt?"

Steiner shook his head. "Not according to Kyne. But until the *Zimnyaya Ledi* took over the city's Dark Caste, she was. Check the next page."

Telinov did so. "Most of these purchases have been in the last four years."

"The same time as the rise of the *Zimnyaya Ledi*. But here is the thing. You remember the possible *Zimnyaya Ledi*-Society connection?"

"*Aff.* Kyne could never prove it."

"One of the two smaller guilds she bought out was the Gray Lotus Guild. Kyne believes it was a Society front and can trace some Society activity to it."

"I can see his suspicions. What else?"

"The next page."

Telinov turned the page and looked at the photo of a man, clearly an Elemental. "Name?"

"Yama. Background is even sketchier than Satinka's. He is listed as a senior laborer supervisor, but the only thing he supervises is Satinka. He was first noticed around the time the Winter Lady started consolidating power."

"Looks dangerous."

"Kyne thinks he is Satinka's chief enforcer."

"Good. What else do you have?"

Steiner pointed to the folder. "Kyne really dug deep for this. Next page."

She turned the page. "A list of purchases." She flipped back several pages, then flipped forward to the page. "These are not listed with the Red Willows transactions."

"Because the goods are not being bought by the Red Willows, but four different Free Guilds, two of which are suspected *Snezhnyye Siroty* fronts, while the other two exist only as names on a form. Kyne traced some of the money to accounts under Satinka's control."

"That is an excessive amount of supplies for personal consumption. The Grand Council made it clear that hoarding is a criminal act."

"Together, *aff*, but not separately. Each purchase is enough to keep a JumpShip and several DropShips supplied for three months."

Telinov nodded. "And two of the companies are nothing more than paper. Where are the shipments going?"

"No idea. They were sent to different systems, claimed by people with the right paperwork, then those people and the cargoes vanished."

"Supply stockpiling, as if they are planning to hide or—"

"Escape," Steiner said, leaning forward.

Telinov scratched her chin in thought. "It is thin, but Kyne may be on to something. I want to find everything about these two suspects and the supplies. Give him access to everything and assign him help."

CHAPTER 13

"I've good news and bad news," Stas said.

Stas and three of his "friends" were sitting around an old conference table in a small room off the weapons cache's main control room. Garmen sat at the head of the table, Wymer behind and to his right.

Stas had contacted Garmen a week after the first meeting. Several days later, Garmen's Point had picked up Stas and the others and taken them out to the cache. The other three were as old as Stas, and he had vouched for all of them. "They're old Wolves like me," he had told Garmen as they sat in back of the truck. "Started lives as warriors, but for one reason or another, they ended up as techs." He introduced the two men as Cuinn and Matteo, and the woman as Grazia.

The four of them had spent the last month inspecting and checking every single 'Mech, spare part, and piece of equipment in the cache, eating combat rations and sleeping in 'Mech cockpits. They rarely spoke to any of Garmen's warriors, instead preferring their own company.

"Bad news first," Stas continued. "Only four of those 'Mechs are anywhere near combat-ready right now—the *Supernova*, *Stone Rhino*, *Sentinel*, and *Firefly*. The rest need major work."

"And the good news?"

"All the spare parts and equipment are here. We can fix 'em all up."

"How long?"

"Six months to a year, with the four of us and your warriors' help. If you want this done any quicker, we need more people."

"I do not want to alert the Hammer and Fists."

"I see." Stas leaned back. "I think you should tell us everything. Like why we are here in a Wolf weapons cache. You've never said you were a Wolf, but I can tell."

Garmen glanced at the other three, then back to Stas. "You trust them?"

"With my life. We're ghost wolves, as you put it."

"You can refuse my request—"

"You want us to perform a suicide strike." The tone was flat, and Stas's eyes narrowed.

Garmen was silent for a moment. "*Aff.*"

"What is the target? The Hall of Khans?"

"*Neg.* The Space Control Center in Katyusha City."

Stas raised an eyebrow. "Tell us everything."

Garmen nodded. "I am Star Captain Garmen Kerensky, and I have been tasked by Khan Vlad Ward with a mission of utmost importance."

He told them everything. The four listened in silence until the end.

Stas narrowed his eyes. "Do you have any MechWarriors of your own?"

"Three, but they are needed elsewhere."

"I see. So, you need eleven more MechWarriors, *quiaff*?"

"*Aff.*"

"Do they all have to be Wolves?"

After several seconds of thought, Garmen shook his head. "If they are MechWarriors, that will be good enough. But they cannot know about our mission."

"That will not be a problem. There are plenty of people like us who have an axe to grind with the so-called Grand Council. Too many lost everything because of the Khans' arrogance and shortsightedness. Just because we aren't warriors doesn't mean we don't hold grudges."

"It will be, as you said, a suicide mission."

"Most of us have nothing left to lose, and you've given us an opportunity to make a difference." Stas smiled. "It's time the Grand Council faced a few vengeful wraiths for their actions."

CHAPTER 14

CENTRAL SECTOR
KATYUSHA CITY
STRANA MECHTY
CLAN HOMEWORLDS
26 AUGUST 3075

Star Colonel Gavril Mikino listed to Kyne's presentation, his dark gray eyes narrowing as the analyst laid out what he had uncovered about the *Snezhnyye Siroty*. When the analyst had finished, Mikino sat back and glowered at him. "I do not like what I am hearing, but I also cannot dismiss what you are saying out of hand. How certain are your conclusions?"

"I stand by them, Star Colonel," Kyne replied.

Mikino nodded and shifted his stare to Steiner. "Do you feel the same?"

"*Aff*, sir. Warrior Kyne's codex speaks for itself, and the evidence is hard to dismiss."

The Elemental turned his head to look at Telinov. "Star Captain?"

Telinov nodded. "I agree. The *Zimnyaya Ledi* is a threat that needs to be removed. The reports that the gang's enforcers, these Shadow Knives, are being trained in advanced military tactics cannot be ignored."

"Agreed. The question is who is training them?"

"I think the man calling himself Yama is responsible," Steiner said. "Our inability to dig up anything on him is suspicious in itself, and his habit of vanishing for days at a time cannot be easily explained."

"Satinka?"

"She's more visible, as she is a Guildmaster. But there are times when she also vanishes, and we cannot account for her whereabouts."

Mikino leaned forward and steepled his large, thick fingers in front of his face. "Bhu, alert the Katyusha Keshik. I want these two found and detained for questioning. It is time we got to the bottom of this *Zimnyaya Ledi* and her minions. And do it quietly. This Winter Lady seems to have ears and eyes everywhere. I do not want to alert her to our intentions."

"Understood, sir."

The Star Colonel rose to his feet. "Solid work, Warrior Kyne. Keep digging. If these two suspects are linked to the *Zimnyaya Ledi*, I want to know about it."

Kyne's head bobbed in acknowledgment. "*Aff*, sir."

CHAPTER 15

NORTHEAST SECTOR
OLD KATYUSHA
STRANA MECHTY
CLAN HOMEWORLDS
30 AUGUST 3075

The buzz of a perscomm brought Garmen out of his doze. He opened his eyes, ignoring the drab bedroom he was in, and reached for the device on the nightstand. "Yes?"

"Evac!" Wymer growled. "Eyes say Fists are converging on your location! They have your names and descriptions!"

Garmen snapped fully awake as a surge of adrenaline shot through him. "Time?"

"Two minutes!"

Garmen reached over and slapped Satinka on the shoulder, jolting her awake.

"What?" she demanded.

Garmen was already on his feet and grabbing his clothes. "Niyol says the Katyusha Keshik are on their way to detain us."

Satinka muttered a curse under her breath and leaped out of bed. Ninety seconds later, they were dressed and ready to leave.

"We are ready," Garmen said into his perscomm.

"Head for the back of the hotel," Wymer said. "The Point will meet you there."

"Copy and out."

They left the room and stepped out into the hallway. The hotel was a shabby, four-story square building in a run-down part of the sector, used mostly by transients. Instead of turning right to the elevators, they turned left, toward the emergency stairwell, moving in sync without saying a word.

They were only a few meters from the stairwell door when they heard the elevators doors open behind them.

Garmen turned and saw several Katyusha Keshik troopers step out into the hall. "Go!" he shouted, shoving Satinka with one hand while drawing his pistol with the other. The sidearm bucked in his hand several times, and bullets flew at the white-clad officers. Most missed, but two of the heavy rounds slammed into one trooper's vest with enough force to knock him down.

Garmen ran, continuing to fire. The troopers returned fire, bullets ripping into the walls, floor, and ceiling around him. He felt one bullet graze his right calf and another round gouge across his stomach. He ignored the pain and fired off the rest of his magazine.

Gunfire ahead of him made his look in the direction he was running. Satinka had reached the emergency door and was shooting past him with her own pistol in a two-handed grip. He heard a cry of pain from behind but did not slow as he slammed his free hand into the panic bar, flinging the door open.

Satinka followed him out onto the landing and looked at his bloody shirt with a critical eye. "You okay?"

He nodded, ignoring the throbbing pain as he ejected the empty magazine and slapped in a fresh one. "Down."

They started down the stairs. They had only reached the second floor when they heard the door below them slam open and boots pounding up the stairs. Garmen glanced over and saw more Katyusha troopers coming up the stairs, trying to trap them in a pincer. "Door!" he snapped, reaching out and grabbing the fire-door handle.

"Grenade!" Satinka replied, pulling a concussion grenade from her clothes. She pulled the pin and tossed the small canister down the stairs.

Garmen darted through the door, Satinka close behind him. They raced down the hallway as the concussion grenade in the stairwell went off.

"Direction?" Garmen shouted.

"End of the hall!" she shouted back.

Garmen punched Wymer's code into his perscomm. "Evac is hot! We're coming out high!"

"Understood. ETA, thirty seconds."

They heard the elevator doors open ahead of them, and a quartet of troopers stepped out into their path. With a roar, Garmen slammed into them, knocking two of them down. He kicked one in the head and stomped on the second one's chest. He spun in time to see Satinka slap her pistol across another trooper's face, while the fourth one was curled up in a ball, clutching his groin.

"Go!" she shouted.

They ran toward a door at the end of the hall. Neither one slowed as they lowered their shoulders and hit the door together. The door exploded inward, and they both stumbled into the room. Satinka swung her pistol around to cover the doorway. "Window!"

There were two windows in the unoccupied room, and a quick glance told Garmen both windows overlooked the rear alley. He grabbed a chair with both hands and hurled it through the nearest window. The sound of shattering glass mixed with a half-dozen shots from Satinka's pistol. The Keshik troopers' return fire from the hall forced her to duck out of the doorway.

"Go!" he shouted, stepping away from the widow and raising his own pistol.

As he fired several rounds down the hall, Satinka darted over to the window and used her pistol's muzzle to clear away the glass still left in the frame. "Clear!" she shouted, then leaped through the window.

Garmen stepped out of the doorway, took out his own concussion grenade, yanked the pin, and threw the grenade through the shattered doorway before leaping through the window after her.

As his feet hit the ferrocrete and his knees protested the landing, there was a dull *crack* as the grenade went off in the hallway. He rose to his feet as a wide truck roared toward them, taking up most of the alley. It slid to a stop several meters from them.

Ziven leaned out of the driver's window. "Get in!"

The pair ran to the back of the truck, where Gada and Dewi waited with assault rifles. As Garmen and Satinka reached the truck's rear doors, Dewi fired off a long burst over their heads, which drew a scream of pain from somewhere beyond the broken window. Dewi stepped back, changing magazines as Gada stepped forward and fired off shorter bursts at the window.

Both Garmen and Satinka scrambled onto the truck as Dewi dropped a smoke grenade and dove in after them. Gada leaped on board, shouting "Go! Go! Go!"

The truck roared down the alley, Dewi throwing additional smoke grenades out the rear doors while Gada raked the hotel's windows overlooking the alley. The truck shot out across the street and into another alley.

"We need to ditch this truck!' Satinka yelled. "And quickly!"

"Wymer is already working on it," Dewi replied.

Ziven made a hard left turn that threw all four people in the back around like dice in a cup. The truck accelerated, and the rear doors flapped open and closed like they were caught in a high wind.

Gada held up a hand indicating he was intently listening to something. "Copy, Iron," he said. "ETA is one minute." He looked at Garmen. "Wymer has another vehicle and is waiting for us."

Garmen nodded. "We'll head for the cache and access the situation." He suddenly felt tired, not physically but mentally. Niyol's frequent complaint echoed through his mind: *We have become Bandit Caste. We are turning away from the warrior's path and becoming criminals.*

He was beginning to think Niyol was right.

CHAPTER 16

CENTRAL SECTOR
KATYUSHA CITY
STRANA MECHTY
CLAN HOMEWORLDS
6 SEPTEMBER 3075

"It has been a week," Star Colonel Gavril Mikino said, his tone deadly quiet.

"Yes, sir," Telinov replied. "Their complete disappearance indicates a level of sophistication not usually found in the Dark Caste."

"Any explanation on how this Satinka and Yama escaped?"

"We think they were warned at the last minute—they must have picked up the raiding force's radio transmissions. They escaped as the Katyusha troopers were moving in. Most of the injured officers have already returned to duty, and we are changing our radio codes to prevent this from happening again."

The Star Colonel leaned forward, his expression stony, and combined with his Elemental mass, made him look like a statue given life. "I do not need excuses, Star Captain. I need results. What about Satinka's organization?"

"Vanished, like their leader. We have contacted other star systems, alerting them to be on the lookout for any Red Willows Guild ships, but none have been reported in the last two days. We have arrested a few low-level members, but they do not know anything."

"What about the *Zimnyaya Ledi*?"

"She and the rest of the *Snezhnyye Siroty* are in the shadows. The Katyusha Keshik has raided a dozen known Dark Caste operations and found nothing. We cannot discount the possibility that the Winter Lady has sources inside the Katyusha Keshik."

Mikino's expression hardened further. "I do not like that idea, Star Captain."

"Neither do I, sir," Telinov said. "I suggest we filter the intelligence we share with the Katyusha Keshik and use Ebon Keshik troopers for any time-critical raids."

Mikino nodded slowly, then leaned forward and stared at Telinov. "I do not care how you do it, I want these people found! Is that understood?"

"*Aff*, sir."

"Get going."

Telinov saluted and left her superior. Outside, Sergis Steiner was waiting for her. "Well?"

"He wants Satinka and Yama found yesterday." They began walking down the hallway. "Have Kyne work up a list of possible targets we can hit that would hurt the *Zimnyaya Ledi*'s organization. We need to get on top of this quickly. I do not like this situation at all, Sergis. It smells like three-day-old fish."

Steiner shook his head. "We are still shorthanded."

"I will submit the request for more personnel and equipment, but there is no telling how long it will be."

"We will do our best."

Telinov looked at him. "We need to do better than our best. The Grand Council has little patience these days."

"We cannot create something out of nothing."

"I know. But I want every rock overturned, every possible lead tracked down. I want these people, Sergis. I do not care how you do it, but I want them."

Steiner sighed. "'A temporary assignment to the Ebon Keshik,' they said. 'It will look good on your codex,' they said." He shook his head. "Give me a battlefield and an enemy I can shoot at any day."

"Hold onto that thought," Telinov said. "If this goes the wrong way, we may be doing just that in a Trial of Refusal."

CHAPTER 17

CHERNYY FOREST
NOVY TERRA
STRANA MECHTY
CLAN HOMEWORLDS
16 NOVEMBER 3075

"The news is not good," Satinka announced.

The weapons cache was more than a place to store weapons; it was a small base, designed to house up to a hundred people. It included a conference room, which had become the core of both the *Snezhnyye Siroty* and the Spatha II operations. Garmen sat at one end of the table, Satinka the other, while Garmen's Point Commanders, Wymer, Niyol, Stas, Cuinn, and Grazia sat on both sides.

The last two months had been difficult. His escape with Satinka from Katyusha City had been tense but without incident. Only stopping long enough to bind Garmen's minor wounds and for Satinka to send a warning message to her people, they used several stolen vehicles to lay a false trail to the Southwest Sector, then slipped out of the city and hiked two days through the forest to reach the cache. Both keshiks had put out arrest warrants for Satinka and "Yama," citing a long list of crimes, some of which were actually true.

Satinka looked around the table. "I've had three different sources confirm the *McKenna's Pride* is being prepared for the Trial of Annihilation against the Steel Vipers—a full crew, weapons load, and aerospace fighter complement. Also, the Grand Council has assembled six naval Stars for the trial. The

Steel Vipers have consolidated their remaining forces on New Kent, and the ilKhan wants to finish them once and for all."

That set off muttering around the table. Garmen let it go on for a few seconds, then said, "Enough. Spatha II is on hold."

"What if the *Pride* is destroyed or damaged?" Ferko growled.

"Then it's damaged or destroyed," Satinka said. "We can't do anything about that. But it's likely ilKhan Banacek will not risk the *Pride* in battle. He wants to use it as a symbol in the Trial of Annihilation against the Vipers, to bring the Great Father into the matter. The *Pride* will return, and we'll wait for the right time to strike."

"What about the *Zimnyaya Ledi?*" Adair asked. "How much longer will the Hammer and Fists scour the city for her?"

"As long as they need to," Satinka replied. "Balbas has four body doubles for me, but he's using them only for the most critical meetings."

"How is the organization holding up?" Garmen asked.

"As well as can be expected. The Hammer and Fists have hit a dozen of our operations, but they didn't arrest any of the major players, and the low-level people don't know anything. Balbas knows what to do."

Garmen looked at Stas. "How is Pilum proceeding?"

Operation Pilum was the name given to the attack on the SCC. What had started out as a simple diversionary attack had become more of an operation than Garmen expected. He had left the planning details to Stas, with help from Balbas.

"Good," Stas replied. "Most of the 'Mechs are combat-ready, and the rest will be finished in a couple of weeks. Training is slow going, as there have been a few arguments among the Wraiths."

Garmen frowned. Despite the fact they were living in the same place, there was little contact between his and Stas's people. As far as most of the newly dubbed "Retribution Wraiths" were concerned, Garmen's people were hired thugs tasked with guarding the cache, while Stas was in overall charge. The MechWarriors, all who looked old enough to be *solahma*, were a mix of former Wolves, Jade Falcons, Ghost Bears, Smoke Jaguars, Fire Mandrills, Steel Vipers, Ice Hellions, and even a Burrock.

"Are they going to be a problem?"

Stas shook his head. "I know them. Once they are out on the battlefield, they will be all right. It's just nerves and knocking off the rust."

Garmen nodded and looked at Satinka. "Status on the escape plan?"

"The guild's still gathering people and supplies," she said. "But they have to do it slowly, to avoid attracting attention. I have a trusted associate, Quartus, overseeing that part of the operation. The ships are using multiple IDs to keep the authorities guessing, but I don't know how much longer that tactic will work."

"Tell them to keep a low profile for now. Anything else?"

Silence answered him, and heads shook around the table.

"All right," Garmen said, "you all know what to do. Let us get to it."

CHAPTER 18

The air around the cache's conference table held something Garmen had not felt in a long time—hope.

"Are you sure?" he asked Satinka.

She nodded. "My sources confirmed it. The *Pride* jumped into the system three days ago and should be back in orbit around Strana Mechty within the week."

"How long to get your people ready?"

"Six weeks for Quartus to get word out, gather supplies, and move them all to the rendezvous point. The *Gray Mist* can be in place at the zenith jump point by then."

Garmen nodded. "Third week of March, then?"

"Make it two months," Wymer said. "We are having a hard time finding the last of the supplies."

"Two months it is," Garmen said. "We only get one shot at this—a couple more weeks will not hurt us now. Any objections?"

He saw a little life flow back into his warriors. His Point Commanders sat a little straighter, while Stas looked relaxed. Niyol seemed stressed but relieved. Satinka looked thoughtful, probably trying to decide what to send in her messages to her people. Wymer remained watchful.

"I want the assault training increased," Garmen continued. "This time, I want Satinka's auxiliaries and techs as part of the exercises. I want three full assault run-throughs every day—morning, afternoon, and evening."

There were a few groans, but Garmen's glare was enough to silence them. "I want full combat gear, Elemental suits—as realistic as we can make it, short of actual zero-G and bloodshed. Stas, if any of your people ask what we are doing, tell them we will be attacking some Katyusha Keshik precinct stations as a diversion for your attack."

Stas nodded. "They will accept that."

"Anything else? No? Good. We start tomorrow."

Garmen leaned on the rail and stared at the 'Mech in their bays. They looked fresh and ready to go, each painted in a mix of white, gray, and black. Each one had a ghostly human head painted on the chest.

"Beautiful, *quiaff*?"

Garmen turned to see Stas standing a couple of meters away. The last year had cast off some of his age; he was still old, but he now looked like the warrior he had once been. He had lost weight, stood ramrod straight, and cut his hair short. A clarity and sharpness had returned to his eyes, and he had stopped using contractions.

"*Aff*, they are."

"You are concerned," Stas said.

"I have much to think about."

"Does that include sending warriors on a suicide mission?"

Garmen looked back at the 'Mechs. "It does."

Stas walked over and leaned on the railing next to Garmen. "Is it because you are sending us to die, or because you are not leading the attack?"

Garmen exhaled slowly. "Both."

Stas nodded. "Dying as a warrior is the one thing I thought would never happen for me."

"But no one else will recognize you as warriors."

The older man snorted. "Being a warrior is more a state of mind than a caste assignment, and the state of mind is more important. Something the present Grand Council has forgotten." He grinned. "We do not care if anyone else recognizes us as warriors—we *are* warriors, and we will die as warriors. After we are dead, we will not care."

He looked at Garmen. "Your mission, Star Captain, is making our sacrifice worth it. A warrior whose death makes a difference between success and failure is a worthy sacrifice."

"It still does not feel right to me."

Stas snorted. "You asked us to fight, and we could have taken that offer or left it. We took it without blinking." He looked out at the 'Mechs. "We were less that *solahma*—not even fit to be cannon fodder—but you have lifted us to that level and given us a path to die as warriors. That is all we could have asked for."

He slapped Garmen on the back. "I have been more alive this last year that I was in the last twenty-five. I have not craved a drink the entire time. You gave us all back something we had been missing—pride in ourselves. And through that, we found the strength in comradeship we had been missing for years. For that, we thank you."

Garmen nodded. "You are welcome."

Stas pushed himself off the rail. "I am going to get something to eat. One thing I did not miss as a former warrior was field rations, but now I am not sure I can eat anything else." He walked away with a swift stride.

Garmen stayed where he was until he felt someone else leaning on the rail next to him. He looked over to see Satinka there.

"You looked troubled," she said.

Garmen looked back at the 'Mechs. "I have much to be troubled about."

"When was the last time you were outside?"

"When we arrived."

She raised an eyebrow. "You've been in here two months without stepping outside?"

"I had no need to."

She shook her head. "You're a warrior, not a burrock. They're looking for me more than they are you, but I still go out to meet Balbas weekly."

"How are your people doing?"

"They are still loyal, but the hiding and constant moving is wearing on them. But they will be ready when the time comes."

"Good."

She placed a hand on his arm. "We will succeed. You will return the Great Father's body to Terra, where he belongs."

"After so long, after so many problems and roadblocks, I am worried another issue will rise to stop us."

"Then you will find a way to overcome it, just like you have before."

He nodded. "I am tired."

"Tired of us?"

He shook his head. "No, you are the one of the things that has kept me going these last five years. I am tired of sneaking around, avoiding the Grand Council's minions, and fighting the frustration that has been nearly as constant in my life as you."

"Thanks, I think."

He shook his head. "But am I still part of the society I grew up and was trained to defend? The last five years has shown me a side of Clan society I do not like. I read all of Niyol's reports on this so-called War of Reaving, and the destruction of the Fire Mandrills, Ice Hellions, and Steel Vipers."

"That is the Clan way. The strong survive, the weak die."

He looked at her. "Then how do you explain the Society? They subverted the Coyotes, then used biological weapons to kill warriors with certain genetic markers, and they twisted genetics to produce abominations that were a mockery of the warrior caste. Because of them, millions died, and they caused destruction on a scale not seen since the Great Father's death! We call the Great Houses of the Inner Sphere barbarians, but after this, who are the real barbarians?"

He looked out over the BattleMechs arrayed below him. "Warriors are supposed to be the guardians of Clan society, yet how many people died simply because they were in the way of a warrior's target? When did orbital bombardment become a viable tactic? When did the use of biological warfare and unauthorized experimentation become part of the Way of the Clans? How can we still claim to be superior to the Inner Sphere when we use tactics they do not?"

Satinka sighed. "First, nothing that happened out there in the last six years is your fault. You didn't create those viruses, order an orbital strike, or execute a single person. When everything else exploded into chaos, you and your warriors stayed on task, no matter what obstacles were thrown at you. You failed once, but didn't walk away. Khan Ward will not blame you for taking this long, especially after you show him Niyol's evidence."

He snorted. "That is something I have avoided thinking about. With the HPG network still in shambles, there has been no way to contact him. Does he think we have failed? Did he send another team to reclaim the Great Father's body?"

Satinka shook her head. "There is zero chance of any Clan Wolf team reaching Strana Mechty in the last five years. While your warriors have been planning and training, my people have been watching commercial shipping."

He looked at her. "And?"

"And it's a fifth of what it was five years ago. Nearly half of the Free Guilds no longer exist, and most of those left will have to either merge or perish. Any newly arrived JumpShip from the Inner Sphere will stick out like a sore thumb, and any Wolf WarShip that appears in Clan Space would be hunted down and destroyed long before it could reach us." She put a hand on his arm. "You've come this far. Now you have to see it through to the end."

"What about you? You and your people are fleeing from everything you have known."

"You're not the only one who does not recognize this new society, Gar. There's too much suspicion everywhere, making it difficult to open or reclaim markets. Most of my network is either gone or taken over by other groups. The authorities are actively hunting me, and I cannot show my face in Katyusha City without being arrested. My people are also being targeted, and there are rumors the Grand Council is planning to put the remaining Free Guilds under their full control. If we stay, we will either suffocate under the Grand Council's heel or risk arrest and execution. There's nothing left for us here. Better to take our chances in the Inner Sphere."

"We do not know what is going on in the Inner Sphere. It could be much worse."

"Yet that is where you're going. If you can take a chance, so can we."

"You may be disappointed."

"Then I'll be disappointed. I'll get used to it."

"What about those who choose to stay behind?"

She smiled. "I'm leaving the *Zimnyaya Ledi* behind. Balbas will continue running the organization in my place. He's smarter and more ruthless than I am, and the Winter Lady will be a perfect cover for him to hide behind. He will keep the keshiks busy." She grabbed his arm. "Enough brooding. You need to get out and enjoy the outdoors."

"It is near midnight."

"Perfect for stargazing. Come on, let's see some stars."

Muttering, Garmen allowed her to pull him away from the railing.

CHAPTER 19

LABORER QUARTER DROPPORT
KATYUSHA CITY
STRANA MECHTY
CLAN HOMEWORLDS
5 APRIL 3076
0507 HOURS

Near dawn, six cargo trucks rolled up to the DropPort's front gate. The guard, a bored and tired-looking Elemental, stepped out of the gatehouse and walked up to the first truck. "You are early."

Satinka shrugged from the driver's seat. She had short dark hair today, and one side was shaved. She handed the guard a clipboard. "Delivery order."

The guard took it and scanned the forms on it. "One moment." He walked back inside the gatehouse.

"I hope this works," Garmen muttered from the passenger seat.

"It'll work," Satinka replied, both hands on the steering wheel. "My people know what they're doing."

The guard returned a minute later. "All right. South Pod, Pad Fourteen. The *Honor* is scheduled to lift off in two hours."

"We will be done before then."

The guard nodded and stepped back as the gates opened. Satinka guided the truck through, and the other five followed.

Garmen waited until all six were past the gate before he keyed his radio. "Six to all Points, we are in. Stand by to execute Able on my word."

As the convoy passed between rows of warehouses, the last truck stopped long enough to disgorge Nokomis's Point and a *Tenevyye Nozhi* squad, who disappeared into the darkness. Their task was to quietly take out any perimeter guards around the landing pad.

The convoy continued on at a slightly slower pace to allow Nokomis's warriors time to get into position. There were still a few signs of the damage the DropPort had taken five years ago—a few burn scars, cracked and fire-blackened ferrocrete, and a few pieces of debris too large to do anything with other than move them out of traffic. Briefly, Garmen thought about Marsali, her Point, and the *Botany Bay*'s crew, with nothing to mark their passing.

Nothing except the completion of this mission.

Satinka made a left turn and in front of them was the South Pod, six landing pads arranged in a half-circle. The *Lion*-class DropShip *McKenna's Honor* sat on Pad Fourteen. Garmen counted thirty people around it, most of them laborers loading cargo. Ebon Keshik guards were on duty around the perimeter, but none wore Elemental armor.

One of the guards waved them down. Satinka came to a stop next to him.

"Why are you here?" the guard asked.

"Cargo for the *McKenna's Pride*," Satinka replied.

"I was not informed of additional cargo."

Satinka sighed and handed the guard the clipboard. "Chief Technician Acis knows. Where is he?"

The guard waved toward the bunker off to one side as he stared at the clipboard. "Over there."

"Tell him we have arrived."

The guard growled and spoke into his radio. "Chief Tech Acis, Point Commander Kilby. I have unscheduled, late-arriving cargo. Driver says you know about it." He listened, then replied. "Understood." He looked up at Satinka. "You the convoy leader?"

Garmen leaned over so the guard could see him. He had shaved his head and allowed a mustache and goatee to grow out. "I am," he said in a rough voice.

"Chief tech wants to see you."

"*Aff*. Tina, get us over there."

Satinka led the convoy over to the bunker. As soon as the trucks stopped, Garmen hopped out with ease, and banged on the side of the truck as soon as his feet hit the ground.

He walked toward the bunker. The bunker was barely a story high, with meter-thick walls and a hatchway with stairs leading down. At the bottom, a second hatchway led to a glass-enclosed office space to the left, while a large open area lay to the right. Beyond this area, hallways went left, right, and straight ahead.

He spotted Acis in the office, looking nervous. He walked in and looked around. "Looking for Chief Tech Acis," he growled.

Acis spun to face Garmen. "I-I-I am Acis," he stammered.

"Got cargo for the *Pride*. The Point Commander said I had to talk to you."

"Of course. We can talk in here." He motioned toward a door, and Garmen followed him into a small office.

As soon as the door closed behind them, Garmen said in his normal voice, "The *Zimnyaya Ledi* sends her regards."

Acis started trembling. "You are from her?"

"Of course."

"My debt will be fully cleared?"

"She gives her word. Is that not good enough?"

The tech nodded jerkily. "W-what do I need to do?"

Garmen reached into his jacket and pulled out a pistol. "I want you to call everyone on the landing pad—laborers, guards, and the ship's crew—into the bunker."

"Y-you don't need that!" Acis stammered, his eyes locked on the pistol. "I said I would cooperate!"

"Relax. When the Ebon Keshik interrogates you, you can tell them the truth, that you were forced to do this at gunpoint." He pointed the pistol at Acis. "Now, call everyone in."

Acis nodded and went to the door.

0518 HOURS

Several minutes later, when the laborers, guards, and the *Lion*'s crew started filing in, Garmen turned to Acis. "Where is the main communications panel?"

"End of the central corridor. The communications equipment room is on the right, the computer room and electrical panel are on the left."

"Good." Garmen whispered into his radio, "Six to Three, status?"

"Perimeter guards eliminated," Nokomis said. "Bodies are out of sight, and we are on watch."

"Copy, Three. Six to all Points, execute Able."

Outside, three of the trucks' rear doors opened, and most of the Spatha strike team jumped out. Along with Garmen's three Points were four squads of *Tenevyye Nozhi*, all dressed in dark-green field uniforms, flak armor, visored helmets, and boots. Under Adair's direction, they stayed in the shadows while the crew and laborers from the landing pad entered the bunker.

As soon as the last of the personnel had gone inside, the two remaining trucks drove away from the bunker, heading for the DropShip.

Led by Adair, the strike team charged the bunker entrance. While a *Tenevyye Nozhi* squad stayed outside on guard, the rest charged down the stairs and into the bunker's assembly area. The guards closest to the door were quickly overwhelmed, disarmed, and struck down with fists or rifle butts. The invaders moved into the bunker, pointing assault rifles at anyone they did not know. Shouts of "Hands up!" and "Put down your weapons!" rang through the bunker.

From the office, Garmen watched. "Time to establish your innocence," he said to Acis.

"What, I—"

Garmen lightly slapped him, and the man collapsed like a broken toy. "Sorry, but you should look like you suffered."

He stepped out, pointed his pistol at the ceiling, and pulled the trigger. The shot echoed in the room and all eyes went to him. "Anyone still standing after five seconds is dead!"

Most of the people dropped to the ground as if they had been shot. Three Ebon Keshik warriors still standing were immediately gunned down. Everyone else dropped to the floor. The office staff, except Acis, were herded into the assembly area with the rest and forced to lie down.

Garmen walked forward. "Face down, hands on your head, and legs crossed! We will collect all weapons and radios.

Anyone not facedown when my people reach you will be executed! Anyone who says anything will be executed! Any resistance, and you and the four people closest to you will be executed!"

A squad of Shadow Knives, Knife Two, began moving through the hostages, collecting weapons and perscomms.

"Knives Three and Four," Garmen said. "Sweep the rest of the bunker for any stragglers. Make sure all air vents to the outside are opened."

"Copy, Six." The two squads split up and left the main room.

Garmen waved Ferko over. "The computers and electrical rooms are at the end of the main hall."

Ferko nodded and waved his Point down the corridor.

"Six, this is Three." Osric, senior Shadow Knife and the one in charge of seizing the *Honor*, called out over the radio. "Objective secured."

"Good. Six to all Trucks, execute Baker."

"Copy," Satinka said briskly. "Executing Baker."

Garmen watched his people continue confiscating radios and weapons from the hostages. After five years of frustration, Spatha was finally underway. But there was no time to relax; they were now committed.

Ten minutes later, Satinka called. "Ice to Six. Baker complete." That meant all of the civilians were aboard the DropShip. "Charlie is a go?"

"*Aff.* Charlie is green."

"Copy. Executing Charlie."

While Satinka's team prepped their DropShip for liftoff, Ferko and his Point returned to the main room. "Everything's wired," he said, looking pleased for once. He gave Garmen the detonator. "When it blows, there won't—*will not* be anything left of that equipment."

"Good. Take your Point and head for the DropShip."

"Right." Ferko motioned to his warriors, and they raced out of the bunker.

The two *Tenevyye Nozhi* squads returned a minute later. "The rest of the bunker is clear," one of the squad leaders reported. "All air vents are open to the outside."

"Stand by." Garmen stood and watched the hostages. All they could now was wait for Charlie to finish.

CHAPTER 20

ANDERY RIVER
TWENTY KILOMETERS WEST OF KATYUSHA CITY
STRANA MECHTY
CLAN HOMEWORLDS
5 APRIL 3076
0523 HOURS

The BattleMechs of the Retribution Wraiths moved along a pair of disused logging trails barely wide enough for them to travel single file, while the old-growth trees on both sides of the trails hid them from aircraft or orbital observation. There was no radio chatter, because Stas had ordered radio silence.

He led the way in a 90-ton *Highlander IIC*. Behind him, the rest of Wraith Star and three members of Revenant Star followed at twenty-meter intervals. Three hundred meters to his left, Phantom Star and the rest of Revenant Star mirrored them. The 'Mechs were all second-line models, but all were fully functioning, thanks to the work put into them over the past year.

Stas had chosen these people because they had all once been warriors who, for one reason or another, had fallen from their Clan's warrior caste. Some were due to misfortune, others from a rival's manipulations, and others by their own actions. All had suffered the fall from grace, and all felt they had been cheated from their life's true purpose.

But they also had something else in common: loss of friends and family to events beyond their control. Stas had lost most of his friends and partner when a WarShip's bombardment obliterated several blocks of a Free Guild enclave while trying to destroy a nearby Blood Chapel. Others Wraiths had lost people, some the same way Stas had, some due to combat or Society experimentation. Still others had been caught in Ebon Keshik sweeps looking for Society members or sympathizers, and few walked out of the Ebon headquarters the same person that had entered.

Sadness and bitterness had become anger, and anger fueled them now. They did not care that they were on a suicide mission: they wanted to punish the Grand Council in a language they understood.

Through the trees ahead, Stas spotted the Andery River. A direct overland march to the city would be folly. The Katyusha Guard, the military arm of the Katyusha Keshik, would move to intercept and either destroy the Wraiths with sheer numbers or delay them long enough to allow a force from Svoboda Zemylya to arrive and finish the job,

"Wraith Leader to all Wraiths," he said over the radio. "Enter the water here. Use passive sensors and switch all weapons to safe before you enter the river. Stay in the center of the channel—that is the deepest part of the river. Keep ten meters separation with the 'Mech in front of and behind you. Be careful—we will be walking with the current."

One by one, each Wraith verbally acknowledged the instructions. Each former warrior was from a dead Clan or one Abjured from Clan Space. They had come together over the last year as a unit through Stas's will and more than a few fists in Circles of Equals. Most would consider these warriors useless, but Wymer had told Stas of a saying he picked up while in the Inner Sphere: *Beware of old people in an occupation where the young regularly die.*

And the Grand Council was about to find out how true that was...

CHAPTER 21

LABORER QUARTER DROPPORT
KATYUSHA CITY
STRANA MECHTY
CLAN HOMEWORLDS
5 APRIL 3076
0534 HOURS

Sixteen minutes later, Satinka said, "Ice to Six, Charlie is green. Liftoff in fifteen minutes."

"Copy, Ice. Six to all Knives. Execute Dog One, repeat, Dog One is a go."

The *Tenevyye Nozhi* guarding the hostages backed away and ran for the entrance, taking the collected weapons and perscomms and leaving just Garmen and Adair's Points in the bunker.

Garmen looked at Wymer and said softly into his radio, "Iron, get the welders."

Wymer nodded and left the bunker. Two minutes later, he was back. "Welders are ready."

"Six to all Points. Stand by to execute Dog Two."

All of Garmen's warriors took out gas masks and put them on. Adair's Point took smoke canisters from their belts and held them ready.

A couple minutes later, Satinka said, "Ice to Six. Dog One is complete. Knives are on board."

Garmen said, "Six to all Points, execute Dog Two, repeat, Dog Two is a go."

As the orders reached his warriors, Adair's Point pulled the pins on the canisters and tossed them among the hostages.

Thick, dense smoke poured from the canisters, and Adair's troopers raced to the hatch and up the stairs. Garmen and his Point backed up toward the hatch at a fast walk, guns still pointing at the hostages as the thick smoke blanketed the area, making it impossible to see anything, but Garmen heard coughing, sobbing, and even some retching.

One by one, each member of Garmen's Point stepped through the hatch. Wymer stepped through, and Garmen took a couple more steps before his boot touched the hatchway's lip. As he stepped over the lip, he pressed the detonator's button. There was a muffled *boom*, and all the bunker's lights winked out from the destruction of the bunker's electrical panel.

Once Garmen was halfway up the stairs, Wymer pushed the hatch shut and locked it. He turned to two of Satinka's men, who wore welding masks and waited with several steel bars and a welding rig. "Do it."

As one of the Knives slid a bar though the hatch wheel at a forty-five-degree angle, Wymer and Garmen went up the stairs and stepped through the outer hatch and into the night air. Wymer closed the hatch almost all the way to keep the welding torch from blinding them.

Garmen caught the edge of the bright light as the welder went to work sealing the hatch frame. "How long?"

"Less than five minutes for each hatch," Wymer replied.

The two men came out four minutes later. "Done," one of them said.

Garmen reached into his pocket and pulled out an armband. It had the emblem of a Steel Viper, and was already torn, to look like it had been ripped off a sleeve. He tossed it through the open hatch. "Seal it."

The outer hatch was closed, locked, and welded shut.

Garmen glanced at the work and nodded in satisfaction. "Six to all Points. Execute Dog Three. Dog Three is green."

The welding equipment was placed in an unrepaired crater near the bunker, along with the confiscated weapons and perscomms. One of the welders opened the fuel valve on the welding tanks all the way, while the other slapped a small charge on the tanks. They ran for the remaining truck in front of the bunker. Dawn was fast approaching, and they needed to be in the air before then.

0547 HOURS

The six northern landing pads were reserved strictly for military DropShips. Three of the pads were closed for repairs, while the other three were occupied by military DropShips undergoing overdue maintenance. No one knew Acis had manipulated the landing-pad repair schedule to force the *McKenna's Honor* to land well away from the other military DropShips.

Technician Imre was working by himself inside the engine room of the *Wild Snake*, a *Carrier*-class DropShip belonging to the Star Adders.

Thirteen minutes before the end of his shift, he glanced around. After confirming he was alone, he reached into his coveralls and took out a fist-sized metal box. He pressed a small button on the side and placed it inside the open panel he was working in, making sure the device was hidden from casual inspection. Once it was secured and out of sight, he closed the panel and picked up his tools. He stretched and waved to a female tech when she appeared in the compartment's hatchway.

"Want to get some breakfast?" she asked.

"Sure," Imre replied. "Breakfast, then about eight hours of sleep sounds good to me."

"Just sleep?" she asked with a grin.

He grinned back. "Maybe not."

CHAPTER 22

WARRIOR'S QUARTER
KATYUSHA CITY
STRANA MECHTY
CLAN HOMEWORLDS
5 APRIL 3076
0618 HOURS

Dawn was breaking when Katyusha Keshik patrol officers Rikka and Katla reached the Andery River. The river ran through the Warrior Quarter, just north of the Central Sector, and was known for its depth and swiftly running current. On occasion, a body had to be fished out of the water, but was still considered a nice place for a walk.

Rikka and Katla were an odd couple. Rikka was an Elemental, two and a half meters of imposing presence clashing with her soft face and short red hair. Katla was the opposite—short, slim, with elfin features, longer blond hair, and a pleasant way of speaking. They were once more talking about their favorite subject—motorcycles.

"What about the Bassa?" Katla asked.

"Pfft," Rikka replied. "Too slow and corners like a drunken, three-legged ghost bear. The T-16 is a better deal."

"The T-16 is unstable at high speeds, plus they take forever to repair! Had one for two years, and it spent nine months of that in the repair shop!"

"With the way you drive, it is no wonder it—" Rikka stopped and looked at the river.

Katla stopped and looked at her partner. "What is wrong?"

"Something under the surface is moving." She pointed. "See?"

Katla saw the wake, and her eyes widened as she saw the ripples turn toward them. "What can that be—"

Something large and gray rose out of the water, close enough for the massive volume of displaced river water to knock them both down and carry them a dozen meters away from where they had been standing.

Katla felt a hand on her shoulder, and Rikka jerked her to her feet. Wiping the water from her eyes, she stared in amazement as a *Highlander IIC* stepped out of the river. It took a couple of strides forward, and another BattleMech, a *Marauder IIC*, rose out of the river and followed the first 'Mech.

Katla looked at her partner, who was staring at the 'Mechs in shock. A *Stone Rhino* emerged from the river next, and it was then she thought about the radio. "Patrol Sierra Three-One to Base! There are BattleMechs coming out of the river! I repeat, BattleMechs are coming out of the river!"

"Are you drunk, Sierra Three-One?" the radio dispatcher said.

"I wish I was, Base," Katla replied as an *Orion IIC* rose out of the river to join the others. "I really wish I was."

0622 HOURS

All the Wraiths that emerged from the river were now advancing into the Central Sector. While using all three Stars to assault the SCC building would have made sense, Stas and Garmen had discussed another plan.

"We need to hit more than just the SCC," Stas had said. "The HPG station and both Keshik HQs also have robust comm systems. We need to cripple their communications, spread out the defenders, and grab their attention. My Star will hit the SCC, as that is the primary target. Phantom Star will attack the Ebon Keshik headquarters, while Revenant Star strikes at the HPG station first, then the Katyusha Keshik headquarters."

They had cleared the plan, and Satinka added to it by pointing out that any force from Svoboda Zemylya could come down hard on the Wraiths from behind. She also had a solution—not a complete one, but one that would make it more difficult for the ilKhan to send reinforcements into the city.

As Stas strode down the street, he changed the radio frequency. "Wraith to Specter. We are feet dry."

"Copy, Wraith," Balbas said. "We are executing Archer."

Stas nodded. "Wraith Leader to all Wraiths. Once we cross the Warrior Sector Square, split up and hit your assigned targets. May the Great Father guide your hands."

"*Seyla*," the Wraiths replied as one.

0625 HOURS

Balbas looked up from the radio. "Execute Archer," he said to one of the *Tenevyye Nozhi* standing near a window.

Half a block away lay the Warrior's Way Bridge, one of seven massive suspension bridges over the Andery River. The bridge connected the Warrior Quarter with the Central Sector and was the most direct route from Svoboda Zemylya.

Balbas walked over to the window as the Shadow Knife pushed the detonator button. From the window, he watched a series of explosions race from one end of the bridge to the other. The entire bridge slowly fell apart, chunks of it plummeting into the river below. Some of the cables strained and snapped, increasing the load on the remaining cables. Then a larger piece separated from the bridge bed and fell into the river with a large splash.

Other pieces followed, and for thirty seconds, it rained ferrocrete, steel, and cables. When it stopped a couple of minutes later, most of the bridge had fallen into the river.

At almost the same time, massive explosions damaged two other major bridges over the Andery River, making them impassable for any military force. Lack of explosives prevented the demolition teams from destroying all three bridges outright or all doing the same to the other bridges, but the ones left were lighter and not designed to handle heavy traffic. Other bridges in the adjoining sectors of Old Katyusha were similar. Any force from Svoboda Zemylya would have to separate and cross multiple bridges, slowing their response time and spreading them out.

Balbas went back to the radio. "Specter to Wraith. Archer is completed. Good luck."

0630 HOURS

The bombs planted on the three military DropShips on the North Pod went off. The bombs were placed to cause the maximum amount of damage with the minimum amount of explosives.

The explosions on the two *Sassanid*-class DropShips, the *Red Fang* and *Black Rattler*, wrecked both engine-control systems, making it impossible for either one to lift off. The explosion on the *Wild Snake* caused even more damage, resulting in an engine fire that took hours to get under control.

While none of the DropShips were destroyed, it would be days before they would be space-worthy again.

CHAPTER 23

CENTRAL SECTOR
KATYUSHA CITY
STRANA MECHTY
CLAN HOMEWORLDS
5 APRIL 3076
0634 HOURS

Alarms woke Bhu Telinov out of a sound sleep. She groaned and looked over at the clock. "Freebirth!" She had only slept for three hours. Groaning again, she sat up and grabbed her perscomm. "Telinov to Control, what is going on?"

"We are getting reports of 'Mechs coming out of the Andery River," the duty officer replied.

"Who is reporting that?"

"A Katyusha Keshik foot patrol made the first report, but we have received several more."

With a snarl, Telinov slapped her bed partner on the hip. "Wake up!"

Sergis Steiner sat up. "What the hell?"

"We may have a problem. Take a look outside and see if anything is coming in from the north."

Muttering, Sergis strode over to the window facing the river and opened the curtain. Dim light flooded the room. He looked out, and Telinov saw him go paler than normal. "I see two 'Mech Stars, maybe more, heading in this direction."

Telinov hurried to the window and stared out over his shoulder. Gray and black 'Mechs were moving through the city from the river. "I can confirm unknown 'Mechs," she radioed. "Has Star Colonel Mikino been informed?"

"*Aff*, Star Captain, but he had an early meeting and is not at headquarters. His ETA is thirty minutes."

"Understood. I will be there in five." She slapped Steiner on the shoulder and turned to grab her duty uniform. "Get dressed. We have places to be."

0639 HOURS

By the time Telinov and Steiner arrived, the control room was in chaos. People were screaming out reports, and the duty officer, an Elemental Star Commander, seemed overwhelmed.

Telinov took one look around and screamed, "*Quiet!*"

The conversation died away.

"We are the Ebon Keshik!" Telinov shouted. "Act like it!" She looked over to one corner and was surprised to find Kyne at the holotable, staring at a computer-generated hologram of the city and advancing 'Mechs.

"Kyne!"

"Yes, Star Captain?" he replied, not looking up from the table.

She strode over to the table. "What do we have?"

"A confirmed Trinary of unidentified 'Mechs. All second-line models, but they look to be in near-perfect condition."

"ID?"

Kyne pushed a few buttons and a close-up of an insignia, a ghostly head, hung above the holotable. They all stared at it.

"Any idea?" Telinov asked.

"Unknown," Kyne replied. "But the identified designs so far are consistent with a Clan Wolf second-line force."

"The Wolves are Abjured," Steiner said.

Kyne shrugged. "That does not change the reality of the identified 'Mechs being consistent with one of their second-line forces. There are also unconfirmed reports of additional enemy forces throughout the city. The Katyusha Keshik is investigating these reports, but the incidents seem designed to sow confusion and delay our reaction to the confirmed enemy BattleMech force."

"Concentrate on the enemy 'Mechs for now," Telinov said. "We do not have the forces to chase after ghosts."

"*Aff*, Star Captain."

"Could it be the Society?" Steiner asked.

"Maybe," Telinov muttered. "But why now?"

"Unknown," Kyne replied.

"Target?"

"Also unknown, but there are a number of possible targets in their path. Our headquarters, the Katyusha Keshik's headquarters, the HPG station, the Space Control Center, Katyusha City Hall, and the Master Genetic Repository. It could be any or all of them."

"Star Captain!" another comm tech called out. "There are reports of explosions on several bridges over the Andery River!"

"Sergis," Telinov said. "Track those reports down."

"On it."

Telinov turned to the Watch officer. "Has the Keshik Guard Command Trinary been deployed yet?"

"*Aff*, Star Captain."

"Call in the rest of the Keshik Guards. Order them to ignore all other reports of enemy forces for now and concentrate on the enemy Trinary. Then, order the streets cleared of all nonmilitary traffic, and all civilians are to head for the shelters. After that, contact the ilKhan and inform him I wish to speak to him."

"*Aff*, Star Captain."

CHAPTER 24

MCKENNA-CLASS DROPSHIP *MCKENNA'S HONOR*
STRANA MECHTY ORBIT
CLAN HOMEWORLDS
5 APRIL 3076
0642 HOURS

On the bridge, Garmen silently watched the sky turn into stars. "How long?"

"Thirty minutes," the pilot replied.

"Star Captain," the communications operator said. "There are reports of explosions in Katyusha City's Central Sector."

Garmen nodded. "Keep me informed." He walked toward the ladder in the back of the bridge and climbed down three floors, past the crew and MechWarrior accommodations, until he reached the main section of the DropShip. The *Lion* normally carried 'Mechs, infantry, and cargo, but the *McKenna's Honor* was assigned full-time to the *McKenna's Pride*, so while it retained the 'Mech bays, they rarely carried 'Mechs, so the bays were often used as extra cargo space.

Today it was filled with people—men, women, and children from Satinka's organization who had decided to come. Two hundred people were sitting on the deck, small bundles of possessions near them. Satinka and Niyol were at the bottom of the ladder waiting for him.

"Well?" Niyol said.

"We are thirty minutes to docking, and Pilum is underway."

"Good," Satinka said. She was now dressed like most of the assault force in a dark-green field uniform and an armored vest, with a green bandana on her head. A laser rifle was slung over her back, and she had a helmet under one arm.

"Have you heard from Balbas?"

She nodded. "Bridges are down and my—*his*—people are flooding the Katyusha Keshik with reports of enemy forces all across the city. It won't take them long to see though the deception, but it might be enough to help Stas complete his mission."

He motioned to the civilians. "How are they?"

"About as well as can be expected. Most have never been off-world before."

Garmen nodded and looked at Niyol, who was dressed the same way as Satinka. "Are you sure the codes are correct?"

"*Aff*. We have years of transmissions and data between the *Honor* and the *Pride*, and we cracked the communications console when we took the *Honor*. They use the same codes in the same order every year."

"Good. I am going to address the assault team. Make sure the civilians are settled in, then join us."

Garmen left them and climbed down another floor and into the hold, where he found his assault team preparing. Adair and Nokomis's Points wore full Elemental armor—where Satinka had gotten them from, he was not sure and never asked. Without their normal short-range-missile launchers, the battlesuits looked less intimidating than they normally did. Instead, each one had a Space Maneuvering Unit attached, for moving about in zero-G. Each suit mounted a micro pulse laser on the right arm, and a grenade launcher on the left arm was loaded with a mix of flechette and smoke grenades.

The rest of the strike force consisted of Ferko and Garmen's Points and six *Tenevyye Nozhi* squads equipped with flak armor, smaller SMUs, and laser rifles. Three teams of techs, also wearing flak armor and SMUs, carried tools and wore sidearms. Unlike the rest, Garmen and his Point wore black overalls with no armor and carried no weapons.

"Ready?" Garmen called out

Adair has his visor up and was grinning. "Been ready for years!"

A chorus of agreement came from the other members of Garmen's Star, and Satinka's people nodded, but said nothing.

"All right, everyone gather around." They clustered around Garmen as close as they could, the Elementals forming an outer ring, while Ferko and Garmen's Points and the *Tenevyye Nozhi* squads formed an inner ring. Garmen was in the center, turning slowly to look at each one as he spoke.

"We are less than thirty minutes from the *McKenna's Pride*. Most of us have been waiting more than five years for this. But remember what happened last time. That time we escaped. But this time we are committed. You all know the plan, and we have rehearsed it until we could do it in our sleep."

He saw determination in all of them, both his warriors and Satinka's people. "But no plan survives enemy contact. Be flexible and ready for whatever the Ebon Keshik throws at us. Keep your people together as you move and make sure of your targets. We hit hard and move fast, and do not get bogged down. Any questions?"

There were none.

"Get ready."

CHAPTER 25

CENTRAL SECTOR
KATYUSHA CITY
STRANA MECHTY
CLAN HOMEWORLDS
5 APRIL 3076
0647 HOURS

The Warrior Sector Square was a large open area, used by the warrior caste for assemblies and Founding Day parades. At the far end, Stas could see the 'Mech-sized statue of the Great Father himself, looking north in the direction of Svoboda Zemylya.

All the Wraiths were in the square when the first of the Katyusha Guard 'Mechs appeared from the south. A white *Hellfire*, a *Glass Spider*, and a *Stalking Spider* advanced into view, and a few seconds later, a *Grizzly* and a *Flashman* joined them on the flanks.

"Attention unknown 'Mechs!" a voice boomed across a dozen radio channels and from the loudspeakers installed flanking the central platform. *"This is Star Captain Steven Zeira of the Katyusha Keshik Guard! Shut down your 'Mechs and surrender immediately!"*

Stas grinned in the cockpit of his *Highlander IIC*. "Why would we do that, Star Captain? We are here to show you what the Grand Council's folly has led to. Now, you can stand aside or you can die here and now. Your choice."

The white 'Mechs responded with weapons fire, targeting the Wraiths' *Orion IIC*. Shells and lasers staggered the 75-ton

'Mech, but Jobina, the former Clan Burrock warrior, kept her 'Mech upright, despite losing armor across her torso and arms.

"Is that the best you can do?" she shouted over the general frequency. "I was hit harder than that in my *sibko*!"

A roar of laughter came from the other Wraiths.

Stas's grin widened. "Wraith Leader to all Wraiths. Let us show them our wrath!"

He targeted the *Hellfire* and fired his Gauss rifle and long-range missiles. The 60-ton Katyusha Guard 'Mech reeled as the hypersonic slug shattered a large section of armor plating just below the cockpit, and the missiles struck all around its legs and lower torso.

Before the Guard 'Mech could fire again, Cuinn and Matteo opened fire on it. The combined firepower of their *Exterminator* and *Supernova* tore through the right side of the torso and found the long-range missile ammo. The 'Mech's Cellular Ammunition Storage Equipment saved it from exploding, but its right arm went flying and smashed into one of the small buildings dotting the square. The heavy 'Mech reeled like a drunk, and its return fire struck nothing but ferrocrete in the square.

Stas kept grinning as he advanced the *Highlander IIC*. Great Father, how he had missed this! He had not felt this alive in decades! "Wraiths, advance!" Again he lined up on the *Hellfire*, firing both his Gauss rifle and long-range missiles.

The fast-moving slug slammed into the center of the *Hellfire*'s chest, smashing through weakened armor and engine shielding alike. Visible heat exploded from the Guard 'Mech, and it staggered again, right as Cuinn fired a second salvo at it. The *Exterminator*'s lasers cut through the *Hellfire*'s remaining torso armor and lanced through the engine. The Guard 'Mech fell over, out of the fight.

"That was *my* kill!" Stas growled.

Cuinn laughed. "Who is keeping count? Besides, there are plenty more targets. This was only a Star. There are two more out there."

Stas looked at the scene before him. The Guard *Glass Spider* and *Flashman* were down, and all Stas could see of the *Stalking Spider* was fragments; he had been so focused on the *Hellfire*, he had not noticed the Guard 'Mech exploding. The *Grizzly* still stood, but looked battered as it backed away from Artemia's *Marauder IIC*. The former Falcon screeched in joy as she continued hammering the Katyusha 'Mech before it ducked out of sight behind a building.

"Wraith Leader to all Wraiths," Stas said. "Split up and head for your targets. Be advised, there are two more Guard Stars out there."

"Phantom Three here," one of the Wraiths called. "I am picking up movement on the right flank."

"Revenant Four, I am picking up movement on the left flank."

"Move it, warriors!" Stas snarled. "If they do not want to fight, leave them alone. We have targets to hit, and the clock is ticking!"

CHAPTER 26

MCKENNA-CLASS WARSHIP SLS *MCKENNA'S PRIDE*
STRANA MECHTY ORBIT
CLAN HOMEWORLDS
5 APRIL 3076
0713 HOURS

"Thirty seconds to docking," the pilot said over the loudspeaker.

The assault team stood clear of the *Honor*'s docking hatch while Garmen stood by the hatch switch. The air hung thick with tension as the DropShip maneuvered into the docking collar.

"Fifteen seconds."

Garmen flipped open the cover protecting the hatch switch from accidental contact. "Stand by."

"Ten seconds. Everything is green across the board."

It seemed longer than ten seconds before the compartment shook with a *thud*. "Docking sequence initiated," the pilot said. "Complete docking in ten seconds. Nine...eight..."

At the pilot's announcement of "Docking complete," Garmen flipped the hatch switch. The heavy hatch rolled opened, revealing the *Honor*'s airlock and outer hatch. The outer hatch rolled open, revealing the *Pride*'s outer hatch.

"Stand by," he said.

The *Pride*'s outer door rolled open, revealing several Elementals. They were dressed in black, but were unarmed.

"What are—" one of them began to say, but stopped when he saw the armored Elementals. The *Pride*'s crew had no defense against the micro pulse lasers, and they died quickly. They floated in the airlock, still and silent.

Garmen looked at Ferko. "Clear the airlock."

As Ferko's Point hauled the bodies out, Garmen nodded to Wymer. "Six to Eyes," he said into his radio. "Activate the Blanket."

"The Blanket is Green," Niyol replied.

Garmen nodded. The Blanket was the *Honor*'s communications system, modified by Satinka's techs into a short-range radio jammer. It would prevent the *Pride* from sending a distress call for a while, but would not last forever.

While Garmen spoke to Niyol, Wymer and the rest of Garmen's Point picked up several crates and floated through the airlock. The crates contained the Point's weapons, armor, SMUs and two techs. Garmen picked up his own crate and followed them through the airlock.

As the *Pride* was in synchronous orbit above Katyusha City, gravity on the ship was nonexistent. He floated down a corridor and followed the others through an open hatch onto a cargo deck. As he placed his crate with the others, he swept the large chamber, noting several cameras and the location of the cargo compartment's workstation in the corner.

They made several more trips, stacking and locking the cargo into the designated shelves in such a way to hide the workstation from the cameras. As soon as the cameras were blocked, Garmen slapped the two crates containing the techs. The hinged side opened, and they floated out. Garmen pointed to the workstation, and the two went to it.

By the time Garmen's Point had made three more trips, the techs were inside the *Pride*'s computer network. Garmen put his crate down. "Well?" he asked.

"Three more minutes to access the internal security system," replied Cassandra, Spatha II's senior tech.

"As fast as you can, Gears."

"We know."

"Six to Eyes, anything from the *Pride*?"

"Nothing."

"Keep on it."

He made another trip to the DropShip and by the time he returned, the two techs were grinning.

"We're in," Cassandra said. "The security camera system is ours."

Garmen nodded, then motioned to Wymer and his Point to armor up. As they opened the crates and pulled out their equipment and weapons, Garmen spoke into his radio. "Six to all Points. Execute Echo. Repeat, Echo is green."

0730 HOURS

With the control of the internal security system, including the security cameras and the hatch controls, the Spatha II team moved into the ship. Alpha Team—Adair and Garmen's Points, two *Tenevyye Nozhi* squads and a team of techs—headed for the bridge to disable the ship's weapons and helm and prevent any distress calls from getting out. Beta Team—Nokomis and Ferko's Points, two more *Tenevyye Nozhi* squads, and another team of techs—headed for the engine room to keep the ship from maneuvering. Gamma Team—the two last *Tenevyye Nozhi* squads, and the third team of the techs under Satinka and Niyol's command—held both the airlock and the cargo hold, where the techs continued hacking away at the *Pride*'s computer system.

Adair's Point led the way, their SMUs allowing them to traverse the corridors and decks quickly. They encountered crew members several times, and the defenders died before they could raise the alarm. The team slowed only long enough to shove the floating bodies into the nearest compartments before moving on.

Alpha Team made it two-thirds of the way to the bridge when alarms screamed and lights flashed.

Garmen scowled. "Six to all Points. What happened?"

"One of the crew hit the alarm before I could shoot him!" Nokomis growled.

"Six to Gears!" Garmen yelled into his radio. "Close and seal all the hatches except the ones between us and our targets!"

"On it!" Cassandra shouted back.

Several hatches slammed shut as they passed, and Garmen heard banging on several others as they flew past. They reached the ladder leading to the bridge, and Adair went up first. He had just stuck his head and upper body through the open hatch when lasers struck him, forcing him to fall down the ladder.

"Are you all right?" Garmen asked.

"Fine." Adair turned toward him, and Garmen saw laser scars across the suit's upper third. "There are two man-portable lasers in front of the bridge doors, offset so they can both fire in either direction. Four or five guards."

Garmen looked at Wymer. "Take Osric's squad and two of Adair's Point to the port-side access. On my signal, fire a grenade spread through the hatch to get their attention, then we will hit them from behind. Once you hear us engage, attack."

Wymer nodded and motioned to the *Tenevyye Nozhi* squad to follow him while Adair directed two of his troopers to go with them. They moved down a cross corridor, Wymer ordering the techs to open the hatches between the port and starboard access points.

"Six to Eyes. How is the Blanket?"

"Still holding," Niyol replied, "but they are trying to burn though the interference. It will not hold for much longer."

"Do whatever you have to, but do not let them get a distress signal out!"

"Understood."

"Any idea on the crew size?"

"Looks like an Elemental security Star and another Star of crew on board—about one hundred and fifty personnel total. We can account for a hundred and twenty of them so far."

"Make sure you find them all."

"We know what we are doing. Eyes out."

"Six, this is Iron," Wymer said. "We are in place."

"Copy, Iron. Start your distraction now."

CHAPTER 27

CENTRAL SECTOR
KATYUSHA CITY
STRANA MECHTY
CLAN HOMEWORLDS
5 APRIL 3076
0732 HOURS

"The Katyusha Guard is giving ground!" the Watch officer shouted.

Telinov scowled, staring at the holomap. Steiner was speaking to a sensor tech a few meters away, his expression serious and angry. Kyne, on the other hand, looked calm, his attention focused on what the map was telling him.

"How bad?" she asked.

"The Command Star, including Star Captain Zeira, has been rendered combat ineffective," Kyne replied, not looking up.

"'Combat ineffective'?" Steiner said, walking over to the holotable. "Zeira and three of his Star are either crippled or destroyed, and the one that still functions is barely mobile!"

Kyne shrugged. "That is combat ineffective."

"What about the rest of the command Trinary?" Telinov asked.

"Beta Guard is in combat with one enemy Star. Gamma Star is shadowing a second enemy Star."

"Shadowing?" Telinov snarled. "This is not an exercise!" She spun to the comm tech. "Inform Star Commander Omid if she does not engage the enemy immediately, I will face her in a Circle of Equals and she will not like the result!"

"*Aff*, Star Captain!"

"Star Captain!" another comm tech shouted. "The ilKhan is on the line!"

Telinov straightened. "Keep an eye on the battle," she said to Kyne, then strode over to an alcove where a comm unit sat. "Patch him through."

IlKhan Hannibal Banacek appeared on the screen. "Star Captain," he said, his tone quiet but his gaze piercing. "What is the situation?"

"An unknown force of 'Mechs, estimated at Trinary strength, has emerged from the Andery River and is pushing south. The Katyusha Guard is engaging them but faltering. We are also getting unconfirmed reports of enemy forces across the city."

"Where is Star Colonel Mikino?"

"He had an early meeting with the Katyusha Keshik's senior commanders in the Laborer Quarter. He is on his way back."

"What do you need from me?"

"My Khan, the rest of the Katyusha Guard is en route, but may not make it in time. The Guard's command Trinary is taking heavy losses, and will not last much longer."

"You are requesting additional forces?"

Telinov straightened to attention. "*Aff*, ilKhan, I am."

Steiner walked over to the comm unit. "Forgive the interruption, ilKhan, Star Captain, but I have an update on the bridge attacks. Engineers report that the three major bridges connecting the Warrior Quarter to the Central Sector are impassable."

Banacek's expression darkened. "I have already dispatched engineers to investigate the other bridges. It is clear the enemy has put a lot of thought into this assault. I would not put it past them to use more *dezgra* tactics." He looked off-screen and nodded. When he acknowledged Telinov again, he said. "I am dispatching both Adder Command Keshiks to the Warrior Quarter's side of the river. Once they clear the bridges, they will assist you."

Telinov raised her eyebrows. "Both keshiks?"

"I intend to crush this foolishness as quickly and ruthlessly as possible. I do not want anyone to think us weak. Hold them off as best you can until we can get across the river. If you will excuse me, I have some other matters to attend to." The screen went blank, leaving Telinov to stare at her reflection.

"The ilKhan wants to use a sledgehammer to kill a marsh fly," Steiner said softly.

She looked at him. "Banacek is in no mood for dissent—from anyone."

Steiner returned her stare for a moment, then nodded. "*Aff*, Star Captain. Message understood."

She returned to the holotable, Steiner following her. Kyne, his expression a mix of puzzlement and worry, was shifting the images from one block to another in rapid succession.

"What is it?" she asked.

"The enemy Stars are splitting up south of the Warrior Sector Square. Beta and Gamma Guard Stars are engaging two of the enemy Stars, but—" He stopped and stared at the images. "The unengaged enemy Star has shifted west. They are going to hit Beta Guard in the left flank."

"Comms!" Telinov ordered. "Inform Beta that they are in danger of being flanked on their left!"

"*Aff*, Star Captain!"

"Kyne, status on the other Guard Trinaries?"

"They are on the move, but are running into civilians fleeing the combat area."

"Order the Katyusha troopers to clear the streets!"

"They are trying to, but the civilians are refusing to follow the troopers' orders."

"Freebirth!"

"Star Captain!" a comm tech shouted. "We are receiving reports of a second unknown 'Mech Trinary in the western part of the city!"

"Get a confirmation on that!"

"*Aff*, Star Captain!"

Kyne tapped a few buttons and scowled. "Star Captain, Beta Guard has been flanked and is now caught in a crossfire."

"*Freebirth!*"

CHAPTER 28

CENTRAL SECTOR
KATYUSHA CITY
STRANA MECHTY
CLAN HOMEWORLDS
5 APRIL 3076
0738 HOURS

The Katyusha Guard *Conjurer* reeled under the combined firepower of Stas's Star before coming apart under the intense pounding. The dying 'Mech fell into a building, ripping the entire side off the structure.

The next Guard 'Mech, a *Thug*, spun toward the new threat, only to get hammered from two different directions as the Wraiths' Phantom Star joined the fight. In seconds, the *Thug* lost both arms, its right leg, and most of its torso armor. The head split open, and a plume of vertical flame indicated the pilot had ejected. The remainder of the Guard Star, a *Phoenix Hawk IIC* and a *Hermes*, quickly retreated to the safety of the surrounding buildings.

"We need to pursue them!" Artemia shouted.

Stupid Falcon! Stas thought. "*Neg*, Phantom Leader. They are no longer a threat."

"We need to finish them off!"

"We *need* to complete our mission. Destroying Katyusha 'Mechs is a means to that effort. If you want to keep fighting, go help Revenant drive off the third Guard Star!"

Artemia's *Marauder IIC* quivered with rage. "Do not tell me what to do!"

"In a few minutes, you will have all the fighting you could ever want. Until then, stick with the mission!"

For several seconds, the *Marauder IIC* went still, then with a snarl of rage, Artemia spun her 'Mech around and strode back the way she came, followed by the rest of her Star.

"It was a mistake putting her in command," Cuinn said over the Star's comm channel.

"Maybe, but this cannot look like an all-Wolf mission. At least Jobina is a competent Star Commander for Revenant, even if she was a Burrock. Let us move to our first target."

"Specter to Wraith," Balbas broke in on the comm. He went silent for a few seconds, long enough for Stas to think he had lost contact with him. "Clan forces are assembling on the far side of the river. We have IDed them as the Adder Command and Quasar Keshiks, and they're checking the undamaged bridges right now."

"Force strength?"

"At least five Trinaries in the Warrior Quarter, but I am getting reports of troop movements in the adjoining Old Katyusha sectors, so it could be all of them."

Stas felt his heart clench. Either keshik outnumbered his force five to one. But both keshiks, manned by the most elite Star Adder MechWarriors in top-of-the-line equipment against his second-line force of has-beens?

He shook the gloom away. He and the others knew this was a one-way mission—Garmen had made that clear to him from the start—and forcing elite warriors to fight them? Well, that was better than he could hope for. "How long do you think we have?"

"No more than fifteen minutes." Balbas was silent for a few seconds. "I could order my people to delay them a little longer."

"*Neg*, you have done enough. Just let me know when the Adders start coming across the river."

"Understood, Wraith. Good luck."

"All right, Wraiths," Stas said over the Trinary channel, "the clock is running. Time to complete our mission."

CHAPTER 29

MCKENNA-CLASS WARSHIP SLS *MCKENNA'S PRIDE*
STRANA MECHTY ORBIT
CLAN HOMEWORLDS
5 APRIL 3076
0740 HOURS

As soon as he heard the explosions above, Garmen counted to five and touched his SMU. He shot through the open hatch and onto the deck above, then touched the controls to arrest his ascent. Both tripod-mounted lasers had swung in the direction of the other hatch. The five guards, all Elementals, were using magnetic boots to anchor themselves to the deck.

One of the defenders spun toward him, but Garmen shot first, his laser burning a hole through the man's face. One of Adair's warriors came up from below, their micro pulse laser filling the corridor with fire. Garmen fired again, scarring another guard's armor but not wounding him. The guard spun toward him, but was cut down by the pulse laser.

A second armored Elemental rose out of the hatchway, adding their pulse laser and grenade launcher. Smoke filled the hallway, and one of the man-portable lasers toppled over as its tripod collapsed. The other tripod laser swung toward Garmen, only to be caught in a crossfire between Garmen and Wymer's teams. The two Ebon Keshik warriors closest to the lasers died next.

The sole remaining Ebon warrior's head swung back and forth, his laser rifle twitching. With an angry yell, he spun toward Wymer's team and opened fire. Osric screamed and clutched his face, and the last guard died in a vicious crossfire.

The teams moved toward each other, weapons ready. Smoke hung in the air, along with the smell of charred flesh.

"How's Osric?" Garmen asked Delma, Osric's second.

"Severe burn across the face. He's in pain, but he will survive."

Garmen looked in Osric's direction as one of the Shadow Knives tended him, spraying burn gel over the injury. The seared skin ran from the bottom of Osric's jaw to the top of his right cheek, but he looked alert and angry.

"Delma," Garmen said, "you're in change of the squad. Osric, with me."

The doors to the bridge were closed and locked. Garmen frowned. "Six to Two, status?"

"Locked out of the engine room," Nokomis replied.

"Six to Gears. Can you open the bridge and engine room doors?"

"*Neg*, Six. Separate system for the high-security areas, and that encryption is more complex."

"How long?"

"Another ten minutes."

Garmen clenched his teeth. "Gears, how much of the *Pride*'s computer system do we control?"

"Most of it."

"Including life support?"

"*Aff.*"

"Do you have the ability to purge the atmosphere from individual compartments?"

"*Aff*, it's used to extinguish fires."

"Purge the atmosphere on the bridge, auxiliary control, engine room—and the tomb."

Cassandra fell silent for a few seconds. Garmen could tell she did not like the order he had just given her. "Copy," she finally said. "Purging life support to those compartments... now."

Garmen looked at his team. "Clear the area and take up defensive position. When they realize what has happened, they will come out fighting. Move."

CHAPTER 30

CENTRAL SECTOR
KATYUSHA CITY
STRANA MECHTY
CLAN HOMEWORLDS
5 APRIL 3076
0744 HOURS

"Gamma Guard Star is combat ineffective."

Steiner glared at Kyne. "Is that all you can say? 'Combat ineffective'?"

Kyne looked up at him blankly. "The term fits, Star Commander."

"Enough, you two," Telinov snapped. She stared at the holotable as the last two surviving 'Mechs of the Star from the Katyusha Guards Command Trinary pulled back. "What is their status?"

"Bad," Steiner replied. "Both have suffered critical damage. One more exchange of fire and they will fall."

"Star Captain! Enemy 'Mechs within sight of the SCC!" the Watch commander called out.

"More enemy 'Mechs are moving this way!" a comm tech called out.

"Where are those other Katyusha Guard Trinaries?" Telinov snarled.

"Still several minutes out."

"Status on the Adder keshiks?"

Kyne touched a few buttons. "Three bridges in the Northeast Sector have been cleared for 'Mech traffic. Three Trinaries of the Quasar Keshik are currently crossing those bridges. Assuming no other problems, they will be here in ten minutes."

A muffled explosion came from somewhere overhead. "What was that?" Telinov demanded.

"'Mechs are firing on this building!" someone shouted.

"Activate the external defenses, evac the building, and get the personnel into the shelters!"

"The SCC is under attack!" someone else shouted.

Another explosion, this one closer, made everyone but Kyne look up. "The HPG station is also under attack," the analyst said, as if talking about the weather.

Telinov's hands tightened into fists. She wanted to be out there, fighting, not stuck sixty meters below the earth. But her position was here. She was responsible for the Ebon Keshik until the Star Colonel arrived.

"Comms!" she growled. "I want the Katyusha Keshik and the Adder keshiks vectored in on the enemy's locations! I want those 'Mechs tracked and any command 'Mechs identified!"

CHAPTER 31

MCKENNA-CLASS WARSHIP SLS *MCKENNA'S PRIDE*
STRANA MECHTY ORBIT
CLAN HOMEWORLDS
5 APRIL 3076
0748 HOURS

The *Pride*'s bridge crew charged out seven minutes after Garmen ordered the atmosphere purged. Before they could get more than a few shots off, they died in the crossfire he had set up. As the last one fell, Garmen's radio said, "Gears to Six! We have control of the secure area hatches!"

"Open the bridge hatches and restore atmosphere *now*!" Garmen shouted. "Alpha, forward!"

With Adair's Point leading, the team swarmed the open hatchway. Wymer tossed a concussion grenade through the open hatch. Several flashes and a riot of noise followed.

Adair's Point charged in, and after a few seconds he radioed, "Clear!"

The rest of the team floated in, followed by the techs, who headed for bridge stations.

"Start disabling the weapons and steerage!" Garmen barked, then called Cassandra. "Gears, have you restored the bridge's atmosphere yet?"

"On it!" the tech replied. "What about the other locations?"

"Leave them off for now. How long to disable weapons and helm?"

"Fifteen minutes or so."

Garmen nodded and waved Wymer over. "Take the rest of the Point to the tomb. When you get there, tell Gears to restore the tomb's atmosphere. Make sure the Great Father is all right, and start clearing the base so the techs can unseal the case."

"On my way." Wymer motioned to the rest of the Point, and they floated out of the bridge.

"Six to Raider," Garmen radioed to the tech team assigned to remove the case containing the Great Father's remains. "Head for the tomb. I want that case off as soon as possible."

"On our way!"

Garmen floated over to the captain's chair. "Who is on sensors?"

"I am, sir," Priam, one of the techs, replied.

"Watch for anyone approaching us. Any movement at all in our direction, I want to know about it."

"*Aff*, sir!"

"Alpha to Beta, status?"

"The engine room is quiet."

"Give it another five minutes, then we will open the doors and restore atmosphere. Six to Eyes, any news from the surface?"

"The Wraiths are raising hell down there. They managed to ravage the Katyusha Guards' Command Trinary, and assaults on the SCC, Ebon Keshik headquarters, and HPG station are in progress."

"The Grand Council's reaction so far?"

"Both Adder keshiks are crossing the Andery River, and the rest of the Katyusha Guard is closing in. The three main bridges are heavily damaged, but not destroyed. Looks like Wraith has maybe ten minutes before he is overwhelmed."

"Let me know when the SCC is destroyed."

"*Aff*, sir."

"Star Captain," Priam said, "a Point of aerospace fighters are headed this way."

Garmen turned to the tech's station. "Any aggressive moves?"

"*Neg*, sir. Normal speed."

"Keep an eye on them."

"*Aff*, sir."

CHAPTER 32

CENTRAL SECTOR
KATYUSHA CITY
STRANA MECHTY
CLAN HOMEWORLDS
5 APRIL 3076
0751 HOURS

Stas slashed his *Highlander IIC*'s lasers into the SCC building, preferring to save his ammunition for the oncoming enemy forces. His Star followed his lead, using their energy weapons to tear into the fortress-like building. Several floors of the twelve-story ferrocrete-and-steel structure were already on fire; thick, black smoke rose into the early morning air.

He stepped back and pointed his torso-mounted pulse lasers at the satellite dishes on the roof and fired. The burst melted multiple holes through the thin metal skin.

"Allow me," Matteo said. He raised both of his *Supernova*'s arms toward the roof and fired his large lasers. The beams burned even larger ragged holes in the dishes.

"Stand back," Grazia snarled. "You are going about it all wrong." Her *Warhammer IIC*'s extended-range particle projection cannons aimed at the building and fired. Both crackling blue beams slammed into one corner of the roof and pulverized a five-meter span of ferrocrete. The roof shifted enough to jar the whole array of satellite dishes out of alignment.

"Cuinn, Matteo, Enda," Stas said, "hit the other corner of the roof on this side. Grazia and I will take out the top-floor supports. And hurry. The Adders are coming."

In less than a minute, the roof collapsed under their combined fire. The satellite dishes slid off the roof and fell a dozen stories to hit the ground as twisted wreckage. Now the top five stories were on fire, and the blaze was spreading down.

"Wraith Leader to all Wraiths. Objective Javelin is complete. Status on other objectives?"

"Revenant Leader to Wraith Leader," Jobina replied, sounding tired but pleased. "Dart is burning, and Arrow has taken heavy damage. Be advised, we are picking up movement all around us."

"Phantom Leader here," Artemia said, anger leaching into her voice. "Objective Spear is damaged, but the defenses are slowing us up."

Stas smiled with satisfaction. The Space Control Center, Javelin, would not be controlling anything for months. Dart, the Katyusha Keshik's headquarters, was on fire and would hamper their reactions. The damaged HPG station, Arrow, would make it difficult to send and receive interstellar transmissions. That left the Ebon Keshik's headquarters, the heavily defended Spear.

"Revenant Star," Stas said, "converge on Spear. We are moving to join you. Wraith Star, move to Objective Spear."

"Understood, Wraith Leader. Revenant is on the move." Jobina sounded happy as she confirmed the order. Only Stas knew how angry she was inside—her former Clan reborn and destroyed before she could rejoin them, most of her friends dead or missing, and her own civilian-caste family no more than a memory. If given an order to destroy Katyusha City, she would have carried it out without a second thought.

Stas changed radio channels as Wraith Star left the burning and broken SCC building behind them. "Wraith to Specter. Pilum is complete."

"Understood, Wraith. Spatha is well underway and still green. Be advised, the bulk of the Adder keshiks have crossed the river and are converging on the Central Sector."

"Understood, Specter. Get your people clear. It is now up to us alone."

"May the Great Father guide you one last time, Warrior."

Stas nodded slowly. He and Balbas were from two very different backgrounds, united in a cold-blooded hatred for the Grand Council's arrogance and incompetence. In the last year of working together, the two men had forged a mutual respect for each other, if not a friendship.

He took a deep breath. "And may he guide you, *chalcas*. May you long continue being a thorn in the Ground Council's side. Wraith Leader out."

Stas tapped a button, eliminating the radio channel from the presets on his system. No matter what happened, there would be no way for the Hammers and Fists to discover the outside help they had received.

Now, he had a last stand to attend.

CHAPTER 33

CENTRAL SECTOR
KATYUSHA CITY
STRANA MECHTY
CLAN HOMEWORLDS
5 APRIL 3076
0757 HOURS

Control center personnel ignored another explosion from above. There were other sounds, gunfire from the defensive turrets around the Ebon Keshik headquarters, but fewer than before as the enemy destroyed the gun emplacements one by one.

"Where are the Adder forces?" Telinov demanded.

"Three minutes out," Kyne said, not looking up from the holotable. "They are joining the Katyusha Guards to encircle the enemy force, then attacking from every direction. The enemy is on the move, consolidating above us."

He tapped a few buttons. "The HPG station is on fire, and the Katyusha Keshik headquarters is destroyed. The SCC is also destroyed, which means we are vulnerable to a spaceborne attack."

Telinov turned to the comm tech. "Notify all WarShips and military craft in-system to be alert for possible hostile forces in space."

"*Aff*, Star Captain."

More explosions boomed above, muffled by the building's thick floors.

"The enemy is massing above us," Kyne said, his fingers tapping swiftly across the holotable's keypad.

"This building cannot take too much more," Steiner growled.

"I am well aware of that, Star Commander," Telinov snarled. "Comms, update the Adder keshiks to our current situation."

"*Aff*, Star Captain."

"There is no way the enemy can escape," Kyne said, then frowned.

Telinov had learned long ago how to read the analyst's expressions. "What is it?"

"The choice of targets is questionable."

"What do you mean?" Steiner asked.

"The enemy wished to hurt us, and they have. But they could have easily launched an attack on the Master Genetic Repository with a high chance of success. However, they have not done so."

"Maybe that is their next target."

Kyne shook his head. "*Neg*, the attack showed anticipation of our reaction, and they knew how to counter it. Yet they chose to attack lesser targets first and not the most important. That does not make sense."

A nearby explosion shook ceiling dust onto the personnel in the control center.

"They are here to destroy us!" Telinov snapped.

Again, Kyne shook his head. "Then they would have hit us first, with the full weight of their force."

"A diversion?" Steiner said. "Something to keep our attention on them?"

"Comms!" Telinov shouted. "Put me through to the head of security at the Master Genetic Repository!"

"*Aff*, Star Captain!"

"Star Captain!" one of the other comm techs called out. "The *McKenna's Pride* has not acknowledged our signal!"

Kyne's eyes widened as something clicked behind them. "They are after the *McKenna's Pride*!"

"It must be some sort of transmission problem," Steiner said. "We do not have time to start jumping at shadows!"

"But it does seem like suspicious timing for something like that to happen," Telinov said. "Closest aerospace fighter patrol to the *Pride*?"

"Two Points of Cloud Cobra fighters, ETA fifteen minutes. A Star of Star Adders fighters are seventeen minutes away. The

CSA *Absolute Truth* is on the other side of the planet from the *McKenna's Pride*."

Telinov nodded. "Inform all fighters of the *Pride*'s lack of contact and direct them to make a flyby to see if they spot anything unusual. Alert the *Absolute Truth* to the situation."

CHAPTER 34

"Sir!" Priam shouted, tearing Garmen out of his thoughts and back to the present.

"What?"

"Two aerofighter Points have suddenly changed direction and are approaching us."

"ETA?"

"Fifteen minutes, less if they hit the over thrusters."

"Six to Iron!" Garmen shouted into his radio. "Status!"

"We have cleared the tomb and have atmosphere. The guards were still at their posts."

Garmen felt a pang of guilt. "Understood. Stay on guard. Alpha to Beta, status?"

"Engine room secured," Nokomis replied. "We have bodies, just like the tomb. We are disabling the engines now."

"Belay that! We have inbound aerofighters, and I do not want to give them any ideas something is wrong!"

"Understood. Holding off disabling engines."

"Six to Iron. How long to remove the Great Father's body from the tomb?"

"I am checking... Six, we have a major problem." Wymer's tone was dark. "Raider says the coffin is not what the plans said they were."

"What? Six to Raider, clarify the problem."

"Sometime in the past," Raider's senior tech replied, "they reinforced the coffin and the deck below it. It's going to take heavier tools than we have, and even then we're talking two to three hours."

Garmen swallowed a curse. "We do not have that much time."

"I know, Six. If I had the right cutting torches, it could be done in ten minutes, but the chances of damaging the body are high."

"Absolutely not!"

"Understood."

"Six," Satinka said. She was still aboard the *Honor*, monitoring the action on the *Pride*. "Those fighters are going to realize something is wrong when we don't answer their hails and they pick up the Blanket's interference. There's another WarShip on the other side of the planet, and we're picking up a dozen aerospace fighters in orbit and in the high atmosphere. We are running out of options."

For the first time in months, Garmen felt doubt creep into his thoughts. To leave without the body would make his mission a failure, the last five years a complete waste,. But to free the body would take too much time. What could they—

"Gar?" Satinka said over their private channel.

"I am busy right now!" he growled. They were so close!

"We can't free the body in time, not without damaging it."

"I know!" He rubbed his forehead, his mind awhirl with thoughts, fears, and doubts. He was a warrior, not a Dark Caste member!

Among the storm of mental images, a memory surfaced of something Satinka had said when she'd discussed her journey to the Dark Caste, years ago. *Why steal the egg when you can take the chicken?*

Take the chicken...

The idea was desperate, but in a sea of chaos, it was the only one with any chance of success. He seized on it with a mental death grip.

"Satinka!" he barked. "I need you on the bridge *now*!"

"What for?"

"We are taking the *Pride* with us!"

Satinka fell silent for a few seconds, and he expected her to object or point out how stupid the idea was. Instead, she said, "I'm bringing the DropShip's crew with me to man the critical systems. We'll be shorthanded, but we can get the *Pride* underway."

"Transfer everyone and everything off the *Honor* and get them onto the *Pride*. If fighting breaks out, they will be safer here."

"'Safe' being a relative term," Satinka muttered, but he heard the humor in her voice. "On my way."

"Hurry!" He pushed himself over to the tech working on the helm. "How long to reenable the helm?"

The tech looked at him in surprise. "Ten minutes. Why?"

"Do it." He turned to the tech at the weapons console. "Reenable the weapons, too." He turned to Adair. "Get your Point to the tomb and relieve Wymer."

The armored Elemental nodded and headed for the hatchway.

"Iron," Garmen said into his radio, "I'm sending Point Two to relieve you. When they do that, get back here. We are taking the *Pride* with us."

Silence greeted him.

"We are *what?*" Nokomis said after a long pause.

"We cannot reclaim the Great Father's body before they discover us, and we have come too far to fail. So, we are going to take the ship and the Great Father with us."

"What about the *Pride*'s crew?" Ferko asked. "They are trapped in sealed compartments for the moment, but we do not have the supplies or personnel to handle them!"

"And I do not like the idea of having that many prisoners aboard," Adair growled. "We could shut down the life-support systems in those compartments, but I do not condone mass murder!"

Garmen turned to the tech manning the systems console. "Yago, you have full control of the life-support system, *quiaff?*"

"*Aff*," replied the tech, an older man with a shaved head.

"And the security system?"

"*Aff.*"

"Can you locate all the people on board?"

"*Aff.*"

"Good, stand by." He stepped back to his chair and found the intercom. "Attention, *McKenna's Pride*'s crew. I am Star Captain Wulfgar of the Steel Viper Ghosts, and we are in charge of this vessel now. Soon I will open a route for you to reach the escape pods. At that time, you will have ten minutes to make your way to an escape pod and eject. After those ten minutes are up, I will purge the atmosphere from this entire ship except for designated areas, and anyone left on board will die. Your choice." He turned off the intercom and exhaled deeply.

"I knew there was still a fuzzy puppy under that hard exterior," Satinka said, her grin audible over the radio.

"I am being practical, Ice."

"It'll be our secret, Six."

Garmen did not bother responding to her. "Six to all Points. I want you all at your assigned locations in thirty seconds, with the hatches sealed. Ice, put the civilians in the cargo hold nearest the *Honor*'s docking collar. In ten minutes, all air on this the ship except your assigned locations will be purged for thirty minutes. Remain where you are until I give the all clear. Six out."

CHAPTER 35

CENTRAL SECTOR
KATYUSHA CITY
STRANA MECHTY
CLAN HOMEWORLDS
5 APRIL 3076
0806 HOURS

Stas, his face bloody, lined up his reticle on an Adder *Timber Wolf* and fired. The Gauss slug struck the 75-ton 'Mech between its right arm and cockpit. His *Highlander IIC*'s missiles struck two seconds later, but the damage spread out across the enemy 'Mech.

The *Timber Wolf*'s return volley ripped into the *Highlander*'s already ravaged armor, and the flash of lights and the sudden wave of heat that hit told Stas his engine shielding had taken even more damage.

For their last stand, the Wraiths had claimed a small park across the street from the heavily damaged Ebon Keshik headquarters. The combined forces of both Adder keshiks and the Katyusha Keshik had hit them from all directions, and the vicious fighting had taken a toll on both sides.

But the odds had been against them from the start. There were too many fresh enemy OmniMechs with full ammo bins, each one piloted by an elite warrior. No quarter had been asked or given by either side, and the park had quickly become a wasteland.

"They are pulling back!" Matteo shouted.

"Consolidate our position!" Stas ordered. "Check ammo and damage!"

A glance at his readouts told him everything he knew. The *Highlander* was heavily damaged, the left leg barely more than a skeleton, and his heat gauge spiked high into the red. He looked at what was left of the Wraiths. Only seven of his command still stood, all shambling wrecks but still ready to fight. Fifteen Adder and Katyusha Keshik 'Mechs lay in ruins around them, along with two dozen shattered Elementals, clear evidence the Wraiths had not died easily or quickly.

His eyes fell on Artemia's shattered *Marauder IIC*. The former Falcon had died as a true warrior, surrounded by three dead Adder 'Mechs and several Elemental suits, her last transmission a scream of defiance. A dozen meters past that lay what little remained of Jobina's *Orion IIC*, destroyed by multiple Adder 'Mechs even as she had smashed her autocannon into the cockpit of an Adder *Executioner* and fired. Cuinn's *Exterminator* had fallen to Stas's left, its ravaged cockpit evidence of the savage fight.

Farewell, my friend, he thought. *The rest of us will not be far behind.*

Then across the radio, a voice said, "This is ilKhan Hannibal Banacek to all enemy combatants in Katyusha City. I offer one chance to surrender."

Stas adjusted his comm frequency to reply. "IlKhan, I am Star Captain Stas, of the Retribution Wraiths. As far as we are concerned, you and the *Grand* Council can go to hell. You were supposed to be the protectors of Clan society, yet you have managed to destroy it. You allowed millions to die, and for what? You needed an object lesson, ilKhan. A reminder of what your arrogance and pride has led to."

Banacek was silent for a moment. "You are insane."

"*Neg*, we are warriors again—wraiths that will haunt you and the Grand Council from now until the end of time. We will linger just beyond your sight, at the edge of the light, but we will be there. Remember us as shadow and spirit, mocking you from the darkness."

"Will you surrender?"

"Of course not!"

"We will crush you."

"You have already taken everything from us—our friends, our families, our lives. We have nothing left to live for. You want us? You will have to come get us."

"Do not expect mercy from us, *stravag*."

Stas laughed. "Do not expect us to die easily, ilKhan. No matter what you do, we will face death as warriors, and you cannot take that from us."

"Here they come," Grazia said.

The Adders charged into the park, their fire intense and concentrated. The Wraiths returned fire, ignoring damage, heat, or any attempt to preserve themselves. Several more Adder 'Mechs went down, but the incoming fire was relentless and overwhelming. The Wraiths died, falling one by one, until only Stas remained standing.

The heat inside his cockpit boiled the sweat from his skin, and he hovered on the verge of blacking out. Gritting his teeth, he lined up a shot on an Adder *Night Gyr* and fired his last Gauss-rifle round and SRMs. The 75-ton 'Mech's side exploded as one of Stas's shots detonated the remaining autocannon rounds. As the *Night Gyr* fell flat on its face, the Adders turned their full fury on Stas.

There were no Wraith survivors.

CHAPTER 36

The tension on the bridge was thick as the techs grimly went about enabling the battleship for combat once again. Several of the *Honor*'s crew with JumpShip experience arrived, along with a balding, skeleton-thin older man wearing an amused expression and a jumpsuit that looked as old as he was.

"Star Captain Kerensky," he said in a pleased tone. "I'm Merchant Quartus. Guildmaster Satinka sent me up here to help."

"You know anything about running a WarShip?" Garmen asked.

"*Neg*, but I captained a dozen JumpShips over the years, and know my way around a few more. No combat experience to speak of, but I know my JumpShips."

"Engine room to bridge!" an unfamiliar voice said over the intercom. "We are ready down here!"

"Helm!" Garmen barked. "How much longer?"

"Two minutes!" the tech shouted.

"Weapons?"

"Thirty seconds!"

"Yago, lock down every single hatch that does not lead directly to the escape pods. Stand by to release the crew on my mark."

"*Aff*, sir!"

"Priam, what are those fighters doing?"

"They just made a pass and are turning to make a second one."

Garmen tapped his radio. "Six to all Points! You have one minute to get to your safe locations before we seal the hatches and purge the atmosphere!"

Satinka shot onto the bridge, grabbing a support to arrest her movement. Niyol was a few seconds behind her. "The civilians are on board and in the cargo hold!" she shouted.

Garmen exhaled slowly. "Satinka, take command."

She stared at him. "Me? I sent Quartus up to take charge."

"Shouldn't the Star Captain be in command?" Quartus asked.

"I don't know anything about JumpShip operations! You two do! I need you to get us underway!"

Satinka grinned. "Sure, Gar." She looked at Quartus "Want to be my XO? I'd feel better if you were here to back me up."

He smiled at her. "Of course, my dear. It will be my honor and pleasure."

Garmen nodded. "Niyol, get the holotable back there up and running. I will be with you in a minute."

"On it."

"Those fighters are making a slow pass," Priam said in a hushed tone.

"Three to Six!" Nokomis said. "Engine room is secured, and the hatches are closed and sealed!"

"Yago," Satinka said, moving toward the center of the bridge. "Start purging the atmosphere in all unoccupied compartments."

"*Aff*, sir!"

Wymer and the rest of Garmen's Point came onto the bridge.

"Find a seat," Garmen said to them.

"Two to Six," Adair said. "Tomb secured and hatches sealed."

"Knife Five to Six," said one of the *Tenevyye Nozhi* squad commanders. "Cargo hold secured and hatches sealed."

"Helm is back on line!" the tech yelled. He moved clear of the helm, allowing the pilots, Fayette and Cronan, to take his place.

Garmen gripped the arm of the captain's chair and keyed his radio. "Six to all Points. Merchant Satinka is in command of the *Pride* until I say otherwise. Merchant Quartus is the executive officer. Keep me informed, but follow their orders unless I countermand them."

A chorus of acknowledgments followed, but Garmen felt uneasy. For the first time in years, someone else was in command, and he was unused to the feeling. He turned to Satinka. "One last thing and the command is yours."

He turned to the tech manning the security and damage-control systems. "Yago, open the hatches to the escape pods and release the crew. Seal all other hatches."

"Opening hatches and releasing crew."

Garmen thumbed the intercom. "Attention crew of the *McKenna's Pride*! Your ten-minute window to escape begins now, so I suggest you not delay! The path to the escape pods is open, but every other access to the ship is locked and sealed! If I see any attempt to access the rest of the ship, I will purge the atmosphere in your area, and you will die. Wulfgar out."

He looked at Satinka. "The command is now yours."

She nodded solemnly and moved to the captain's chair. "Engine room, stand by."

0825 HOURS

The *Pride*'s crew expulsion went smoother than Garmen expected. Once released, the crew dashed for the escape pods. From the security cameras, Garmen counted 112 crewmen and Elementals as they climbed into twenty-one escape pods and ejected into Strana Mechty's orbit.

Satinka nodded as the second wave of pods launched. "Okay, people. Make ready to break orbit."

"What course?" Fayette asked.

"Zenith jump point. I want us at one G as quickly as possible, but expect orders to boost acceleration on my command."

"*Aff*, Captain!"

"Yago, carry out the Star Captain's order. Seal all compartments behind the last of our departing guests, then shut down all life support on the ship, with the exception of the bridge, engine room, the cargo hold, and the tomb!"

"*Aff*, Captain!"

"Course laid in!" Cronan shouted.

"Execute!"

Satinka looked at Garmen as gravity began asserting itself for the first time since they had boarded the *Pride*. "So far, so good."

Garmen's expression was grim. "Still have a long way to go."

CHAPTER 37

CENTRAL SECTOR
KATYUSHA CITY
STRANA MECHTY
CLAN HOMEWORLDS
5 APRIL 3076
0823 HOURS

"The *McKenna's Pride* is launching escape pods," Kyne announced.

Telinov looked at him in puzzlement. "What?"

"The *McKenna's Pride*—"

"I heard you the first time. Why is it launching escape pods?"

"Unknown, Star Captain."

Telinov turned to the one of the comm techs. "Has the aerospace patrol made contact with the *McKenna's Pride* yet?"

"*Neg*, Star Captain. Some interference near the *Pride* is making communications impossible."

"Do they report any signs of damage or evidence of a problem?"

"They report no sign of any exterior damage, and the ship's distress beacon has not been activated."

There was a commotion at the control room doorway. Telinov stiffened as she saw both the ilKhan and Star Colonel Mikino enter. Mikino was wearing a dirty and worn Ebon Keshik dress uniform while the ilKhan wore a MechWarrior's suit. They scanned the room and grabbed everyone's attention before heading to the holotable. Both Telinov and Steiner stiffened to attention, but Kyne continued working, staring at the data the holotable was displaying.

"Star Captain," Mikino said, his brow furrowed. "What is going on?"

"The *McKenna's Pride* has fired up its engines," Kyne announced, "and is still launching escape pods." He peered at the holotable images. "I am detecting atmosphere venting from the *Pride*."

"What is going on, Warrior?" Banacek asked Kyne in a deep but mild tone.

"IlKhan, I think someone is trying to steal the *McKenna's Pride*."

"What?" Mikino growled. "How?"

"The *McKenna's Honor* docked with the *Pride* ninety-five minutes ago, on a regular supply run. A force could have slipped on board that way."

"Impossible!"

"So is an enemy Trinary appearing in the middle of the capital, Star Colonel," Banacek said. "Right now, I would dismiss nothing out of hand. Alert all spaceborne forces."

"That will be difficult," Kyne replied. "The SCC had been rendered ineffective—it was one of the targets the enemy went after." His expression changed. "Wait, that makes sense."

"What?" Telinov asked.

"Why the SCC was targeted. They destroyed it to hamstring our space defense."

"Why?" the ilKhan asked. "Why would they try to steal the *McKenna's Pride?*"

"Orbital bombardment?" Steiner said, his suggestion sending a shiver down Telinov's spine.

"Great Father, I hope not," Banacek said, his cool tone at odds with his words. "Warrior, any sign the *Pride*'s weapons are being readied for action?"

"No, ilKhan. There—the *McKenna's Pride* has broken orbit," Kyne said without passion.

"Show me," the ilKhan ordered.

Kyne touched a few buttons, and the holotable's image changed to show Strana Mechty, with icons representing the different spacecraft and their vectors. One icon, labeled sls mckenna's pride, was moving away from its normal orbit.

Banacek stared at the image for several seconds. "Order the *Absolute Truth* to break orbit and pursue. Are there any other WarShips in-system?"

Kyne pressed a few more buttons. "The CCC *Brimstone* and *Nebulous* are on their way in from the nadir point, but will not arrive in orbit for another three days and are too far in-system to make a jump."

"Star Colonel, update the *Brimstone* and *Nebulous* to the situation."

"*Aff*, sir," Mikino said, moving to the nearest comm tech and relayed the order.

"Warrior," Banacek said, "can you tell where the *Pride* is going?"

"I will need a minute."

"IlKhan," Telinov said while they awaited Kyne's analysis, "did any of the enemy MechWarriors survive?"

Banacek shook his head. "They all fought to the last breath."

"Have they been identified yet?"

"I have a team of the Adder Watch identifying the bodies. When they are finished, they will pass the identities along to the Ebon Keshik for further investigation."

"The *Pride*'s course is toward the zenith point," Kyne said. "Its current acceleration is approaching one G."

"Any other WarShips due to jump in-system soon?" Banacek asked.

Kyne's fingers flew across the holotable's control panel. "The CSA *Sovereign Right* is due to arrive in four days."

"Where is it now?"

"Recharging at the Huntress system's nadir jump point."

Banacek nodded. "In addition to pursuit, the *Absolute Truth* is to contact the *Sovereign Right* and inform them of what has happened. On my orders, the *Sovereign Right* is to jump in and intercept the *Pride*."

"*Aff*, ilKhan."

"I also want those escape pods recovered. Warrior, how many aerospace fighters are currently in orbit around Strana Mechty?"

Kyne stared at the images for a few seconds. "Three full Stars, but they are scattered."

Mikino rejoined the discussion. "The *Brimstone* and *Nebulous* have been alerted."

Banacek nodded. "Star Captain, order the fighters to pursue and disable the *Pride*'s engines."

"Why would anyone steal the *Pride*?" Mikino muttered.

"I think they intended on stealing the Great Father's body," Kyne said.

"Why?"

"It is useless to speculate about it now," Banacek said. "When we have retaken the *McKenna's Pride*, we can ask the survivors—if there are any."

CHAPTER 38

MCKENNA-CLASS WARSHIP SLS *MCKENNA'S PRIDE*
STRANA MECHTY SYSTEM
CLAN HOMEWORLDS
5 APRIL 3076
0829 HOURS

"New contact!" Priam yelled.

"Where?" Garmen demanded.

"ID?" Satinka said at almost the same time.

"Large craft—it's a WarShip!"

"Send it to the holotable!" Garmen strode to the back of the bridge, followed by Satinka and Quartus. By the time they arrived, the image was up and displaying a holoimage of Strana Mechty's near orbit. After a few seconds, an vessel icon appeared, and a few seconds later it had a label: csa absolute truth.

"That's not good," Satinka said as she stared at the map. "They're reacting faster than expected."

Garmen looked at the Watch officer. "I need a rundown on the *Absolute Truth*."

Niyol tapped a few buttons. "*Nightlord* class," he said. "The good news is we are larger, with more firepower. The bad news is they have more armor, a full crew complement, and up to a hundred Points of Elementals they can board us with, along with aerospace fighters. If those fighters nipping at our heels slow us down enough, those Elementals will swamp us."

Quartus shook his head. "I doubt there's more than a Trinary of marines on board at the moment. *Nightlord*s only carry that many infantry when they are moving a Galaxy from one place to another."

"That's still enough troops to reclaim this ship," Satinka said. "We'd be outnumbered two-to-one against trained marines."

Garmen felt frustration seep into him. "What are our options?"

"Keep running," Satinka replied. "It's the only thing we can do."

"Agreed," Quartus said.

Satinka turned back to the bridge. "Fayette, increase speed to 1.5 Gs. Priam, I want you to keep a close eye on the *Truth* and the aerofighters. We've taken them by surprise, but as soon as they figure out what we're doing, they're going to be all over us like a pack of hungry ice hellions."

"Can we not use the ship's weapons against the fighters?" Garmen asked.

Satinka turned to face him. "We could, but that would be like a blind man using a sledgehammer to swat flies."

"You have to understand, Star Captain," Quartus said, "naval weapons are designed for use against other WarShips and JumpShips. They're not designed to track something as small and as fast as an aerospace fighter. The only effective anti-fighter weapons we have are the AR-10 missile launchers."

Satinka shouted, "Weapons! Status on the aft missile launchers?"

"Launchers are ready," replied Bran, the tech manning the weapons station.

"How are we on missiles?"

"Full loads—twenty Killer Whales and White Sharks, thirty Barracudas."

"Can you launch them from here?" Garmen asked.

"*Neg.* They have to be fired from the missile stations."

"Which we cannot do right now, because the atmosphere in those compartments has been purged." Garmen sighed. "But if those fighters attack in the next half hour, we are defenseless."

"The *Pride* has plenty of armor," Satinka said. "It'll take more than a few fighters to get through to anything vital, and we only have to last half an hour. Once we restore atmosphere to the rest of the ship, we can get people to the launchers and shoot back. My main worry is the *Absolute Truth*. We have a lead on them, but they will be coming hard after us. If they remain on our tail, we won't be able to recharge at the zenith point."

Garmen sighed. "I did not think of that."

"Your first theft of a naval vessel?"

He glared at her.

Satinka smiled. "That's why you have me and Quartus around." She turned back to the bridge. "Cassie! Start recharging the jump drive at normal rate."

"*Aff*, Captain!"

"Captain! Sensors are picking up incoming aerospace fighters!"

"Understood," Satinka said calmly. "Pipe the data to the holotable!"

Garmen could feel the extra G from the *Pride*'s increasing thrust when he turned back to the table. He stared at the image. "Looks like a mixed Star. First ones will be in range within seven minutes."

Satinka nodded, her expression thoughtful. "We just need to hold out for half an hour."

"I would be more concerned about them sending DropShips after us," Quartus said, his expression serious. "We can shoot those with the *Pride*'s primary weapons, but they have more weapons and heavier armor than fighters and are faster than WarShips. Trying to fight off three or four of them would be—"

Just then, Garmen felt a shift in the *Pride*'s thrust. "What was that?" he demanded.

"Felt like a DropShip detaching," Quartus said.

"The *McKenna's Honor* has detached itself from the *Pride*!" Yago shouted.

"Did it undock, or was it torn off?" Satinka shouted.

"Clean undocking! Someone's on board!"

"How?" Garmen shouted. "Who?"

"I don't know!"

"Helm, what is our acceleration?" Quartus asked.

"1.05 Gs!"

"That sounds like an undocking," the merchant said. "DropShips can be torn off at acceleration at more than one G, but not that quickly."

Garmen scowled. "Satinka, check with the civilians and see if anyone is missing."

"Right." She looked at Quartus. "With the *Honor* away, we can use the comms. Contact the *Gray Mist* at the zenith point. Tell them the pickup is aborted and they are to immediately jump to the rendezvous point."

"Of course."

Satinka moved to the captain's chair while Quartus headed for the unmanned comm station.

Garmen remained where he was, staring at the holoimages. "What is going on?"

Niyol studied the bluish images. "The *Honor* is drawing away a few of those fighters."

"Only a few." Garmen frowned as he watched the icon representing the *McKenna's Honor* change course. "What are they doing?"

"They have increased speed too," Niyol said. "They are up to 1.5 Gs now." He looked up at Garmen. "Sir, I think the *Honor* is going to attack the *Truth*."

"That is insane."

"More like desperation," Satinka said, walking up to the holotable. "Three civilians are missing, all DropShip crew members."

"More fighters are breaking off in pursuit of the *Honor*," Niyol said. "The *Honor* is up to two Gs. Time to interception with the *Truth* is three minutes. It will be within the *Truth*'s weapons range in forty-five seconds."

Satinka frowned. "They won't be able to maneuver at that velocity."

Quartus walked back to the holotable. "What did I miss?"

"The *Honor* is making a suicide run on the *Absolute Truth*."

"The *Honor* has just increased thrust!" Niyol shouted. "2.5 Gs!"

"There is no way anyone could be piloting that ship," Garmen said, unable to look away. "The G-forces would make it almost impossible."

"I think they activated a control program," Quartus said solemnly. "They just programmed in the course and sat back, making minor course corrections as needed."

"But it will make it impossible for them to fire any weapons."

"Oh, they're not going to need any weapons," Quartus replied, his expression sad. "In this case, the *Honor* is the weapon."

Garmen stared at him. "They are going to ram the *Truth*? That is insane!"

The merchant shrugged. "So was Tyra Miraborg's actions twenty-odd years ago—a one-in-a-million chance that changed history."

Garmen frowned. A single Inner Sphere pilot had delayed the Clans' advance into the Inner Sphere by flying her aerospace fighter into the Wolf Clan WarShip *Dire Wolf*, just as a Grand Kurultai was taking place on board, resulting in the death of ilKhan Leo Showers. The ilKhan's death had forced the Clans to return to Strana Mechty to elect a new ilKhan, a process that delayed the invasion for a year and gave the Inner Sphere nations time to rebuild their forces, develop new tactics, and form alliances. The Clans returned, but the yearlong delay had cost them their momentum.

"The crew on the *Honor* are not warriors," Garmen said.

Satinka shook her head. "They may not be warriors, but they are showing a warrior's heart. They are willing to sacrifice themselves to give us a better chance to escape."

"The *Truth* has opened fire on the *Honor*," Niyol said.

Garmen looked back at the holotable. Niyol had readjusted the image to show the confrontation in greater detail. The *Absolute Truth* was firing everything it could at the rapidly approaching DropShip. The *Honor*'s twisting, erratic course made it a difficult target to hit. Several lasers and a couple of autocannon rounds slammed into the DropShip, but it continued closing the distance.

Garmen stared at the image, unable to look away "They cannot last much longer."

As if to prove him wrong, the *Honor* continued its death dance with the *Truth*, taking several more hits, but never slowing, never wavering. A thousand kilometers became five hundred, then 250 kilometers, 100 kilometers. The *Truth* was changing course, trying to bring more of its firepower to bear onto its target.

"*Honor* is up to three Gs!" Niyol said in a hushed tone.

As he said that, the *Honor* was struck by several autocannon rounds and exploded less than two kilometers from the *Truth*. The resulting explosion blasted fragments in every direction, ripping apart a closely pursuing fighter Point, but like a massive shotgun blast, the bulk of the *Honor*'s fragments slammed into the *Truth* at three Gs, smashing and slicing into the battleship's heavily armored bow. As Garmen watched in silence, the remaining fragments of the destroyed DropShip flew past the *Truth,* rapidly expanding in the battleship's wake.

"They did all they could," Satinka muttered.

Quartus nodded. "I hope it was enough."

CHAPTER 39

CENTRAL SECTOR
KATYUSHA CITY
STRANA MECHTY
CLAN HOMEWORLDS
5 APRIL 3076
0857 HOURS

"What is the status on the *Truth*?" Star Colonel Mikino demanded.

Kyne tapped a few buttons. "Its bow armor has taken severe damage, some structural damage, the bow naval Gauss, naval PPC, one naval laser, and both large lasers are either destroyed or offline. Current casualties are seventeen dead, nineteen injured, but that will most likely climb. The *Truth* has slowed down to assess damage and make temporary repairs, but the captain says it can be up to full speed in one hour." He stared at the image and muttered, "Which is probably optimistic."

Telinov felt tired, but she could not leave, and if the reports were correct, she had no quarters to go back to. Enemy 'Mechs had savaged most of the building above. Her stomach grumbled, reminding her that she had not eaten since last night. "What were they thinking?"

"We are dealing with Society fanatics," Mikino growled. The ilKhan had been called away on other matters, leaving Mikino in charge of the pursuit.

"Doubtful," Kyne replied, not looking up from the holotable.

Mikino planted both hands on the edge of the holotable and glared at Kyne. "Are you telling me I am wrong, *Warrior*?"

he growled. He was nearly twice Kyne's height and four times his weight.

Kyne looked up, his expression showing no fear at the Star Colonel's anger. "If there are any Society assets left on Strana Mechty," he said slowly and evenly, "they are not behind this. This was planned by someone with military experience, access to intelligence, and the ability to gather people, train them, and execute this operation. The Society never once demonstrated this level of military ability. The armband we found at the bunker and the thief claiming to be Star Captain Wulfgar of the Steel Viper Ghosts are leads we need to follow up on."

"Star Colonel?" Telinov said. "Kyne is right. We have no evidence that the Society is behind this. We should worry about recapturing the *Pride* right now."

Mikino drew back, his expression still a simmering anger. "Very well. Once the *Absolute Truth* has finished repairs, it is to pursue the *McKenna's Pride* at its best speed—fuel or high Gs are immaterial!"

Kyne looked down at the images on the holotable. "Sir, I should point out that we do not have the SCC's network or processing power. While we can access the satellites and sensor networks, we lack the comm bandwidth or the computers to process the data in a timely manner. That will result in delays on the data we are receiving."

"How bad?"

"Right now, the delay is less than a minute, but it will get worse the more satellites and sensor networks we have to access to track them. I estimate a minimum of several minutes' additional lag for every hour the *Pride* accelerates from the planet, and that does not include the signal-transmission delay."

"What do you need?"

"We could use the *Truth*'s HPG to broadcast data back to us—it would help with our bandwidth by concentrating several data streams. But we currently do not have an operating comm system on-planet that can receive, decrypt, and process military data transmissions."

"What about the Hall of Khans?" Telinov asked. "Can their comm system handle it?"

Mikino scowled. "Svoboda Zemylya's main satellite-dish cluster is still being rebuilt. It will not be ready for another three weeks."

"And the best four comm systems on-planet were the ones the enemy went after," Steiner said. He stood at the far end of the holotable, staring at the images in front of him.

"*Aff*," Kyne replied. "We need a dedicated military-grade comm system to handle the *Truth*'s data transmission."

The Star Colonel's expression darkened. "I see. I will find one." He looked at Telinov. "Status of the DropShips' repairs?"

"The *Red Fang* and *Black Rattler* are still being repaired, but it is at least a two-day job. The techs said whoever planted those bombs knew what they were doing. The *Wild Snake* is going to need weeks—the bomb caused a fire that destroyed most of the engine and the fuel tank."

Mikino nodded. "I need to update the ilKhan. Keep me apprised of any new developments."

Telinov gave him a slow nod. "Of course, sir."

She leaned on the table and stared at the images it displayed as Mikino left. "Who *are* you people?" she muttered.

"Unknown," Kyne replied, not looking at her.

She sighed. "That was a rhetorical question."

"Oh."

Steiner looked up at Kyne. "You are lucky the Star Colonel did not challenge you to a Circle of Equals."

"I do not fear the Star Colonel in formal combat. I have already analyzed several of his previous combat trials and have formulated several counters, should the need ever arise."

Telinov raised an eyebrow. "You have?"

He glanced up at her. "*Aff*. I learned in *sibko* that I would never be the fastest, strongest, or toughest warrior. I learned to fight smart, not hard. It does not matter how good a warrior you are if you have a poor plan and no intelligence."

She nodded. "Do you really think the Society is not behind this?"

Kyne looked down at the holotable. "I told the Star Colonel the truth. There is no evidence the Society is involved, and the operation is not the sort they have executed in the past."

"Why steal the *McKenna's Pride*?" Steiner asked. "What use is it to anyone?"

"I do not think the *Pride* was the main target. I believe they want the Great Father."

Telinov raised her brow at Kyne's conclusion. "You mentioned that earlier. Assuming you are right, how do we start trying to prove that?"

"The bodies of the enemies who attacked us would be a starting point."

She nodded. "You are right. I will expedite their identification."

CHAPTER 40

MCKENNA-CLASS WARSHIP SLS *MCKENNA'S PRIDE*
STRANA MECHTY SYSTEM
CLAN HOMEWORLDS
5 APRIL 3076
0914 HOURS
(JUMP DRIVE RECHARGE TIME REMAINING: 183 HOURS, 15 MINUTES)

Twenty minutes passed in silence. The *Absolute Truth* had just begun resuming its pursuit at 1.5 Gs, but the *McKenna's Pride* had accelerated to 1.75 Gs, opening the gap. The aerospace fighters still harassed them, but their attacks were pinpricks.

From the captain's chair, Satinka looked back at Garmen, who was still standing at the holotable. "It's been half an hour, Gar."

"Go ahead."

Satinka turned back. "Yago, bring back the atmosphere. Main corridors and vital compartments like the gunnery stations first. How long until it's back up to normal levels?"

"Fifteen minutes."

Satinka nodded. "XO, give me the intercom."

"*Aff*, captain," Quartus said, flipping a switch on the comms panel. "You are on."

She grinned. "Attention all passengers and crew of the *McKenna's Pride,* this is your captain. Atmosphere is being restored to the rest of the ship. In fifteen minutes, you can unlock your hatches. Once the atmosphere is restored, Knives One through Four will sweep the rest of the ship for any of the former crew who decided to stay behind. Knives Five and Six, meet technicians Hade and Floyd at the aft missile launchers and start learning how to work the missile launchers. Civilians, stay where you are until we have cleared the ship, then we'll escort you to the crew quarters. Apologies for the extra G—it seems our hosts don't want us leaving quite this soon. Captain out." She looked back. "Good enough?"

"Better than I could have done," Garmen said. "Six to all Points. I also want a count of the dead, and full accounts of all supplies, especially food. Commander's meeting in three hours, Six out."

1216 HOURS
(JUMP DRIVE RECHARGE TIME REMAINING: 180 HOURS, 11 MINUTES)

They used the same conference room where, according to Satinka's people, both Star Adder Khan Stanislov N'Buta and ilKhan Brett Andrews had died within minutes of each other eight months ago—N'Buta at Andrews's pistol, Andrews at the hands of the Adders' then-saKhan Hannibal Banacek. There was no evidence of that violence anymore, but Garmen could not shake the feeling that their ghosts were watching them in silent anger.

Besides Garmen, his Point Commanders, Satinka, Wymer, and Niyol, there were a few additions. Osric, the laser scar covered by a skin patch, represented the *Tenevyye Nozhi*, Cassandra for the techs, and Quartus the civilians. They all sat at the same table the Khans had used, the same place where the Great Father and his staff had sat when they had led the SLDF out of the Inner Sphere three centuries ago. Everyone present was showing the physical strain of feeling nearly twice their own weight due to the ship's acceleration.

"Let us start with the basics," Garmen said. "Food and water?"

"We have a three-week supply," Quartus replied. "And enough combat rations for three more weeks, but I hope we are not that desperate. We also have uniforms, spare parts, and small arms. My people are still searching and inventorying the cargo holds."

"I want a full list before the next meeting. Anything else?"

Niyol nodded. "We have cracked the captain's safe and have all the comm encryption and access codes currently in use."

"What else?"

"We've swept the ship and found no one else," Osric said. "We have thirty-four bodies, all crew members killed in the initial takeover."

"All right. Place the bodies aboard several escape pods and launch them." Garmen looked at Satinka. "What about our pursuers?"

"The fighters have backed off after we destroyed three of them with missiles," she replied. "They're waiting for additional fighters to reach them. As for the rest, we've detected four DropShips lifting off from Strana Mechty and pushing 2 Gs to catch up with us, but it'll take them awhile to be a threat. The *Absolute Truth* is still losing ground, but slower than I would like. We have about an hour-and-a-half lead on them right now."

"Damage to the *Pride*?"

"Some aft armor damage, but nothing too serious."

"Keep an eye on those fighters. I want Hade and Floyd to continue training Osric's squads on our weapon systems, just in case."

Satinka nodded. "*Aff.*"

He looked at Quartus. "How are the civilians?"

"More comfortable in the crew quarters than they were in the cargo hold," the merchant replied. "But high-G acceleration is not something most of them have experienced. I told them to stay close to their quarters and limit activity to the basics."

"What is their mood?"

"About what you would expect for civilians. Most are apprehensive, and a few others are resigned to whatever fate that comes their way. No panic or anger yet, but it's still early."

Garmen nodded. "Good. Let's move on to duty shifts..."

0127 HOURS
(JUMP DRIVE RECHARGE TIME REMAINING: 179 HOURS)

Garmen stood outside the *Pride*'s former officer's mess, now the Great Father's tomb. He had taken a shower, dressed in a fresh black uniform, and was clean-shaven. Steadying himself, he opened the hatch and stepped inside.

Ferko's Point had the duty shift, the four Points rotating the honor every two hours. The five Elementals stood at attention at the four corners of the coffin, with Ferko standing at the foot of the casket. Despite the extra gravity, all five stood ramrod straight, facing outward, their rifles at port arms. They had also cleaned up and wore fresh uniforms.

Garmen walked over to the coffin. General Aleksandr Kerensky lay with his arms crossed over his chest, eyes closed, as if in sleep. His gray command uniform was adorned with medals, more than any warrior Garmen had even seen. A part of him wondered how a man who looked so unassuming could be such a warrior. A piece of ferroglass lay across the top of the coffin, and the sides were flat-finished metallic, adorned with the Cameron Star. To Garmen's left, the viewport that had spent centuries looking down on Strana Mechty was now showing stars.

Garmen felt years of history descend on him. "I wish to be alone for a few minutes," he said in a soft voice. Without a word, the Elementals walked out of the compartment, and the hatch slid shut behind them.

"Grea—General Kerensky," he said, coming to attention. "I am Star Captain Garmen Kerensky of Clan Wolf. I claim blood ties to you through your son, Andery. Your son Nicholas built a new society on the ashes of the old, and for nearly three hundred years, we lived in relative peace. We even returned to the Inner Sphere and reclaimed some of it."

He placed his hand on the ferroglass. "But the society Nicholas created has changed. Clans were destroyed, absorbed by stronger Clans or cast out from the home you found for us. Millions have died needlessly over the last several years, centuries of custom and law thrown to the wayside at the slightest excuse. Clan Wolf, the Clan your sons became a part of, and whose blood runs deep in many of us, has been Abjured from Clan Space."

He took a deep breath. "It is time you returned to the Inner Sphere, sir. Your son swore that one day you would be back on Terra, and that day is sooner rather than later. I have been given the task of bringing you back. The last several years have been spent doing just that. We had not intended on taking this entire ship, but we have no choice. I ask for your patience, sir.

I ask for your guiding hand as we embark on our journey. I ask for your strength to see this through. But most of all, I ask for your clarity. Give me those, and I can get you back to the Inner Sphere. Back home, sir."

He patted the ferroglass, saluted, then turned and walked back to the hatchway. It slid open, and Satinka stood there. She looked serious and a little nervous.

"What is it?" Garmen asked.

"I want to see him," she said.

He stepped back and she stepped inside. As soon as she saw the coffin, she stopped and stared. "It's him," she breathed, walking over to the coffin to stare down at him.

"*Aff.*"

"He...doesn't look like a great man."

"Maybe that was his secret."

"He looks peaceful."

"If there is anyone who deserves peace, it's him."

She nodded. "Do you think we're doing the right thing?"

"I have to think so."

"I know. You've always wanted to do the right thing—it's one of the things I love about you."

"We should leave him and get some rest."

She nodded, and they walked out.

CHAPTER 41

Telinov leaned back in her chair and tried to keep her eyes open. She suddenly smelled strong coffee and opened her eyes to find a cup in front of her. She glanced left and saw Steiner standing there, a plate with a sandwich on it in his other hand. "You need this."

She took both. "Thank you."

"Not a problem, Star Captain."

The conference room next to the control room lacked anything that gave it any character. The walls were bare and beige, the table large, rectangular, and unremarkable. The chairs were high-backed, padded, and tolerable.

"Anything new?" she asked before she started eating.

"Kyne is reviewing the data on the bodies of the enemies."

"The *Pride*?"

"Still accelerating out of the system, heading for the zenith jump point. It has a two-hour lead, and that is slowly increasing. The *Truth* is trying to reinforce its bow and is pushing as hard as it can, but any faster, and their bow could collapse. Kyne says the data delay is now nearly two hours."

"Has the Star Colonel found a comm system yet?"

"Under the ilKhan's authority, he is requesting a mobile HQ from a cache and having it driven here. He hopes to have it set up and ready within twelve hours."

"That is not going to help with getting word out. Any update on how long the HPG station will be offline?"

"At least a month. The ilKhan has ordered both the *Brimstone* and *Nebulous* into orbit and will use their onboard HPGs to send word outside the system."

Telinov shook her head. "What is going on?"

Just then, Kyne rushed into the conference room, his expression perplexed. "Star Captain, may I have a moment of your time?"

"Of course. What is the matter?"

Kyne sat across from her and Steiner. "I have reviewed the data on the dead attackers, and what I am finding does not make sense."

"In what way?"

"Well, all of the bodies identified so far were once all Trueborn warriors who had been demoted from the warrior caste, some more than twenty years ago. None of them were younger than forty, and most were older. All were in the technician or laborer caste, most of them Free Guild members or low-level members of a Clan other than the one they had been born in. Most were reported missing from their jobs between eight months to a year ago."

"What Clan are they from?"

"That is what I do not understand. The dead are from a multitude of Clans, all of which are either dead or Abjured."

"The records of an Abjured Clans are erased," Steiner said.

Kyne shook his head. "Only the public ones. It would be foolhardy to eliminate all records of the Abjured. What happens if they come back? I have no doubt that even the unaltered records of Annihilated Clans are hidden deep in the Khans' archives, just in case."

"Get on with it, Kyne," Telinov said.

"Several dead have been identified as four former Wolf warriors, and the rest are from Clans that have been Absorbed, Annihilated, or Abjured."

"The armband they found at the landing-pad bunker is suggestive," Steiner said. "Also, this Steel Viper Ghosts mentioned by this Star Captain Wulfgar."

"Now I believe it is a ruse to throw us off."

"There has to be a connection between them," Telinov said. "Keep digging, Kyne. Find out how they are connected."

Kyne abruptly stood. "*Aff*, Star Captain." He spun and left the room at a fast clip.

Telinov sighed and stared down at her half-eaten sandwich. "I have lost my appetite."

"Eat it anyway," Steiner said. "No telling when you will get another chance. I will inform the Star Colonel of Kyne's findings."

Telinov picked up her sandwich. "*Neg*, I will do it. You see about getting Kyne some help. He has to be running on fumes, too."

"I will see what I can do."

CHAPTER 42

The next twenty-four hours saw tensions ratchet up among the bridge crew. The pursuing fighters, now supported by several carrier DropShips, had swelled to two full Stars in strength. They made constant attacks, trying to goad the *Pride* into wasting missiles while doing more armor damage, but lost five fighters in the process.

The *Absolute Truth* was still in pursuit, but had fallen five hours behind the *Pride* and continued losing ground. A dozen military DropShips from Strana Mechty had also joined the pursuit, but were still a full day behind.

During that time, Garmen stood watch, slept, ate, and spent several sessions alone with the Great Father. He did not know why, but he found a certain release in talking to the general, voicing feelings he could not express elsewhere. He always felt better when leaving the tomb, ready to do what was needed.

Garmen looked around the conference table. "Does anyone else think this is too easy?"

"Something is going to happen," Ferko said.

"Agreed," Quartus said.

"But what?" Garmen looked at Cassandra. "Any problems?"

The senior tech shook her head. She and her team were exhausted from the extra G and the twenty-hour shifts they were working. "None we can find. The ship is running smooth, and we scoured the computer system for any hidden surprises, but found none."

"Scour the computers again, and I want every compartment swept and checked. Get the civilians to help out. Anything else?"

"Might I make a suggestion?" Quartus asked. "If I were trying to catch us, I would contact a WarShip in a nearby system and have it jump in at the zenith point or a pirate point along our current course, when we are too close to avoid them."

"Then why are we heading toward the zenith point?" Ferko growled. "Why not head off in a random direction and jump when we are far enough out?"

"Habit," Satinka said with a frown. "We hadn't planned on stealing the ship, remember?"

"How many pirate points are we talking about?" Garmen asked.

Satinka picked up the noteputer off the table and her fingers flew across it. After a minute, she looked up. "There are three possible I can see, but I won't know for sure until I sit down and analyze them."

Garmen grimaced. "What would you suggest?" He looked around the table. "We cannot fight a single battleship, let alone two."

"First thing we should do is change course," Satinka said. "Heading for the zenith point is a no longer a viable option."

"That does not get the *Truth* and their friends off our trail," Ferko said. "We cannot slow to a stop to make a jump, not with them only hours behind us."

"There's no need to."

Everyone looked at Quartus, who sighed. "I know a tactic we can use, since this is a WarShip. It's something I would otherwise advise against doing under normal circumstances, considering our crew's lack of experience."

Satinka snorted. "What's normal about stealing the most important Clan WarShip from under the Grand Council's nose?"

"Explain this highly unadvisable tactic," Garmen said.

"It's called a 'running jump.' Basically, the WarShip makes a hyperspace jump without stopping first. It's useful when a WarShip needs to arrive or leave a system in a hurry."

"That sounds insane, "Adair said.

Quartus shrugged. "Not really. It's not easy or simple, and you can't do it with a standard JumpShip, but it's less risky than trying to slow down for a jump. Anyway, the idea is simple enough. You make a jump while at speed."

"What is the catch?" Ferko growled.

"The catch is it's harder to calculate the jump, because you have to account for the WarShip's velocity in addition to all the usual variables. Make a slip in the calculations, and who knows what happens?"

There was silence around the table. "I can think of a few things," Satinka muttered.

"What about our velocity coming out of a jump?" Nokomis asked. "Will that be a problem?"

Quartus smiled. "Not at all. When we come out of the jump, assuming something doesn't go wrong, all our velocity will be gone. The jump-drive controller takes care of that."

"That does not sound too bad," Niyol said.

"It will not be easy." He spread his hands. "But I am a simple merchant, what do I know?"

"Don't let the 'simple merchant' air fool you," Satinka said, grinning. "Quartus here was the best smuggler in Clan Space—he wrote the book on the subject. But he's right. If we change course, it'll improve our chances."

Garmen looked from Satinka to Quartus and back again. "Can we plan such a jump?"

Satinka looked at Quartus, who nodded. "With Quartus's help, yes."

"How do you know of such a tactic?" Wymer asked. "You said only WarShips can use it."

Quartus smiled ruefully. "I was doing business on Atreus about twenty years ago, and the Ice Hellions' saKhan took exception to my presence. He chased me off-world, then sent a WarShip after me, the *Chaos Sailor*. He chased my DropShip all the way out to the nadir point, and along the way, I was a bit...imprudent to radio the *Chaos Sailor*'s captain and question his parentage."

Satinka's eyes widened. "You didn't!"

"Oh, I did. Thought I was being clever. We reached our JumpShip, did a drop-and-lock, and figured we could give the *Chaos Sailor* the slip."

"What's a drop-and-lock?" Niyol asked.

Satinka scowled. "It's when you throw safety and caution to the wind by docking a DropShip to a JumpShip as fast as possible. The JumpShip then jumps the instant the docking collar locks. A highly dangerous tactic that only the insane or desperate would do!"

Quartus shrugged. "I agree it's not something that can be done without a lot of practice and precision piloting, but my crew was both very good and very practiced."

"What happened?"

"Well, we made the jump, but not before I teased the *Chaos Sailor*'s captain one last time. We arrived at our destination, an uninhabited star system. Our JumpShip, which had a charged lithium-fusion battery system, was just getting ready to jump again when the *Chaos Sailor* appeared, ten thousand kilometers off our port bow and with zero velocity! They quickly got underway to come after us, of course, but we jumped away before they reached weapons range. But I never forgot that maneuver, and I made it a point not to insult any more WarShip captains after that."

"So, what do you suggest?" Garmen asked.

"We change course," Satinka replied. "If they do jump a WarShip in front of us, they will be forced to chase us, instead of coming at us head-on."

"All right." Garmen looked at Cassandra. "What is the status of the jump drive?"

Satinka held up a hand. "That brings up another problem—the jump drive."

"What's wrong with it?" Ferko growled.

"What's wrong is we don't have enough time to fully charge the drive before we hit the system's edge. In most cases, it takes at least a hundred and seventy-five hours—a week—to recharge the jump drive. Currently, we are using the *Pride*'s onboard reactor to power the jump drive at a normal rate, but as of right now we're going to hit the minimum safe-jump distance in less than four days."

"Which means...?" Nokomis asked.

"It means we either continue running while we charge at the current rate, which means the Grand Council has more time to call in additional forces, or we increase the charging rate and risk damaging the jump drive."

Garmen looked at Cassandra. "Your opinion?"

"The charge has about a hundred and fifty hours to go," the tech replied. She took a deep breath. "If we had to do it right now, I could fully charge the drive in...twelve to fifteen hours. But I must recommend against that."

"I second her advice," Satinka said.

"And I third it," Quartus said. "Cramming that much energy into the jump drive that quickly is a risk we need not take at this moment."

"How great a risk?" Garmen asked.

"Right now?" Cassandra lowered her head for a few seconds, then looked up at Garmen. "If I were to quick-charge the drive using the fusion engine right now and make the jump attempt at the minimum safe jump distance, one of four things would happen. Best outcome is we jump successfully—I give that about a ten percent chance of happening."

Garmen frowned. "Go on."

"The next best is we lose some or all of the charge—we don't jump and we're back to recharging the jump drive, which means we are in-system longer, which gives the ilKhan plenty of time to hunt us down. I put that at about a twenty-five percent chance."

"That does not sound good," Ferko said.

"It gets worse," Cassandra said. "There's another twenty-five percent chance that we lose the entire charge and damage the jump drive in the process. That means we start again and hope the drive isn't seriously damaged. None of my people have any expertise in repairing K-F drives."

"And the last outcome?" Garmen asked.

Cassandra dropped her head to look at the table. "There's a forty percent chance the jump attempt destroys the jump drive beyond repair, and we are stuck in the system."

The room was silent for several long seconds. Finally, Wymer said, "I suggest we do not quick-charge the drive unless there is no other choice."

"Agreed." Garmen looked at Satinka. "I leave the decision when and if to quick-charge in your hands."

She nodded. "The longer we hold off on that, the better our chances for a successful jump. Cassandra, keep the charging at current levels, but I want your team ready to do a quick charge on my command. I'll give you as much time as I can, but if we have to—"

"I understand, Captain. When you need it, we'll do it."

Satinka nodded. "We'll alter course in twenty-four hours. It'll take me that long to figure out the pirate points on our current course, and a new course that doesn't have any potential pirate points."

"We do not know whether a WarShip is jumping in to intercept us," Nokomis said.

"We cannot ignore the possibility," Niyol said.

"I think we should bet on there being a WarShip," Quartus said. "In any case, changing course is a good idea."

"Agreed," Satinka said. "We've been making it up so far and been lucky. Now it's time to stop reacting and start planning."

"Is that going to cause a problem with the jump calculations?" Garmen asked.

She shook her head. "Between the *Pride*'s nav computer, my noteputer, and Quartus, I should be all right."

"Good." Garmen looked around the table. "Let us get back to work."

CHAPTER 43

Bhu Telinov walked into the Ebon Keshik command center, feeling like she had fought several Circle of Equals in a row. She was tired, sore, and had eaten little more than the sandwiches Sergis had given her in the last two days.

She was unsurprised to find Kyne already at the holotable, working the data as he had since the incident started. Since the *Pride*'s theft, he had been the first one in the morning and the last out at night, assuming he ever left.

He looked up as she approached the table. "Star Captain."

"Kyne," she replied. "What is the latest?"

"The Star Colonel found two mobile HQs and has both set up outside the building. One is acting as a receiver for the *Absolute Truth*'s HPG signal, while the other is acting as a comm link to spaceborne units via the *Brimstone*. The *Nebulous* is holding position to act as an HPG station, sending out alerts to other worlds and staying in contact with the *Sovereign Right*."

"The data?"

"The lag is now manageable. The mobile HQs' computers are not as good as the SCC's, but they are designed to decrypt and route military data." He motioned to the table. "The results you see here are only six minutes old. The *Pride* currently has a seven-hour lead on the *Absolute Truth*. The pursuing aerofighters are now at Trinary strength, with DropShip support, and are stepping up their attacks. The *Sovereign Right* is scheduled to jump in at pirate point B-14 in three hours."

"What about the background on these so-called Wraiths?"

Kyne looked up at her. "I did find one thing in common. They all lost friends and families in the last five years, either by the Ground Council's actions or the Society's. For example, the suspected leader, Stas, lost most of his Free Guild and his partner on a misplaced orbital strike in the aftermath of the second Wolf raid. The evidence leads me to believe he recruited all or most of the others."

"What about the 'Mechs themselves?"

"All are Wolf Clan, probably from a cache left behind when they departed Clan Space."

"So the Wolves are behind this?"

"I have no evidence of that. While the leader was a former Wolf Clan warrior and the 'Mechs are probably from a Wolf cache, the Wolf Clan cannot—" He stopped and stared at the holotable as something flashed to catch his attention. "Interesting."

Telinov felt the hairs on the back of her neck rise at Kyne's flat tone. "What?"

"The *Pride* has change course and is no longer headed for the zenith point."

Telinov moved to the holotable. "What heading?"

Kyne tapped a few buttons. The holotable showed icons representing the pursuit ships and their quarry. "I am analyzing the new course now."

"Where are they going?"

"I am not sure, but it appears they realized the zenith point is not a good idea."

"Freebirth!" Telinov growled as she leaned on the table and studied at the icons. "Can the *Sovereign Right* change its destination?"

Kyne's fingers flew across his touch panel, and he stared at a chart that appeared before him. "They could. However..."

"What?"

"The *Pride*'s new course does not have any usable pirate points near it."

Telinov scowled. "Freebirth!"

Kyne nodded. "The best arrival position is still B-14, but the *Sovereign Right* will be forced to intercept at an angle instead of being right in the *Pride*'s path, as originally intended."

"Freebirth!" Telinov growled. "I will call the Star Colonel."

CHAPTER 44

MCKENNA-CLASS WARSHIP SLS *MCKENNA'S PRIDE*
STRANA MECHTY SYSTEM
CLAN HOMEWORLDS
7 APRIL 3076
(JUMP DRIVE RECHARGE TIME REMAINING: 140 HOURS, 41 MINUTES)

Garmen was asleep in one of the bunks designed for the Elemental guards when an alarm snatched him out of slumber. He rolled out of the bunk, feeling heavy and sluggish from the extra G, and activated the compartment's communication panel. "Garmen to bridge. What is it?"

"Quartus called it," Satinka replied. "A WarShip just jumped in at pirate point Able."

"ID?"

"Not yet, but we should know in a few minutes."

"I am on my way up."

Garmen was on the bridge within ten minutes, and Satinka and the rest of the command staff were waiting for him at the holotable.

"We have identified the WarShip," Niyol said. "It is the CSA *Sovereign Right*. A *McKenna*-Class battleship, just like this one. It should take them a few minutes to get their bearings."

"Good," Garmen said, nodding. "What is the earliest we can jump?"

Satinka glanced at a timer in one corner of the holotable. "We'll reach the proximity point in fifty-six hours, twenty-three minutes."

"Jump plotted?"

"*Aff.*"

Garmen turned to the engineering station. "What is the status on the jump drive's charge?"

"We're at twenty-five percent!"

"And how much damage have those fighters done?"

"Some," Satinka replied, "but WarShip armor is a lot tougher than aerofighter armor. It's the DropShips I am worried about."

"You think they may attack?"

"Two of them are *Sassanid*s," Niyol said. "Even if they are only carrying a partial load of Elementals, if both board us, we will be overwhelmed."

Garmen nodded. "Understood. Keep an eye on both WarShips and the DropShips. Any of them of them make a move, let me know."

CHAPTER 45

CENTRAL SECTOR
KATYUSHA CITY
STRANA MECHTY
CLAN HOMEWORLDS
8 APRIL 3076

"Star Captain?"

Telinov looked across the holotable at Kyne. "What?"

Kyne looked unruffled, but Telinov could see the tiredness in his eyes. He had been analyzing all the data, looking for a way to stop the *Pride*'s escape. "I have found another WarShip we can bring in. The CGS *Lei Kung*. It is currently at Lum, preparing to head to Huntress."

She blinked. "I will tell the Star Colonel."

Goliath Scorpion Khan Ariel Suvorov did not look happy as Telinov followed Mikino into the conference room. Recent rumors spoke of shouting matches in the Hall of Khans over the *McKenna's Pride*, and Suvorov's surly demeanor lent the stories some validity. An aerospace pilot, the Khan looked tiny compared to Mikino's mass, but an air of authority surrounded her.

"Khan Suvorov," Mikino said in a formal tone.

Suvorov folded her arms. "Why do you need to see me, Star Colonel?"

"I have a request from the ilKhan."

"Which is?"

"The *Lei Kung*. It is currently at Lum, *quiaff?*"

"*Aff*, it is." Her words were cold.

"If it were to jump into this system, at a point in front of the *McKenna's Pride*, we could block it from jumping out of the system."

"I see. You are aware that the *Lei Kung* is only three days into its recharge cycle?"

"*Aff*, Khan."

"So you are asking me to order the *Lei Kung* to quick-charge its jump drive, *quiaff*?"

"*Aff*. I would not ask were the situation not so desperate."

The Scorpion Khan nodded. "I will transmit the order. This theft attempt is an attack on all of us, so now is not the time to be stubborn. But in return, I want to be updated on the situation."

"Of course, Khan."

"I will have orders ready to transmit in thirty minutes. Is that satisfactory?"

"*Aff*, Khan. Due to the HPG station being damaged in the attack, we are currently using the *Nebulous*'s onboard HPG to relay information in and out of the system. I will alert them to expect your message."

Suvorov nodded and rose. "I will start right away."

After the Khan walked out, Telinov slipped into a chair and sighed.

The Star Colonel looked at her. "Problem?"

"*Neg*, sir. I just feel we are grasping at straws here."

"Because we are. The *Lei Kung* is our last shot. It *must* succeed."

Telinov nodded. "*Aff*, Star Colonel."

"When was the last time you got any sleep?"

"I—I..." She blinked. "I do not remember."

"Go get four hours of sleep. That is an order. You are no good to the Ebon Keshik, the Grand Council, or the ilKhan if you cannot think straight."

"*Aff*, Star Colonel."

CHAPTER 46

Garmen looked around the conference table and wondered if anyone else was as tired as he. The entire scratch crew had been pushed to the limit, each one doing the work normally done by five or six crew, under a constant 1.75 G.

Since the *Sovereign Right*'s appearance, the Grand Council had increased the pressure on the escaping battleship. The *Right* was coming in hard at a 1.9 G burn, closing the distance between it and the *Pride*. Another Star of fighters, using the *Sovereign Right*'s *Carrier*-class DropShips as bases, added their attacks to the around-the-clock assaults against the *Pride*. The strikes had cost the pursuers seven more fighters, but the *Pride*'s aft armor was thinning out. The *Absolute Truth* remained in pursuit, though it was still falling behind.

"Where are we?" Garmen asked. He looked at Cassandra, whose eyes were closed. "Cassie, the jump drive?"

Cassandra did not react until Osric shoved her. Her eyes flew open in surprise. "What?"

"The jump drive," Garmen said, fighting the urge to snap at her. "Status?"

She blinked. "Oh." She picked up the noteputer in front of her and stared at it for a few seconds. "It's at forty-five percent."

"We're still more than twenty hours from the proximity point," Satinka said. "I recommend continue holding off on fast-charging as long as possible. We still have about a thirty-percent chance of blowing the drive."

"Assuming nothing else happens," Adair muttered.

The words were barely out of his mouth when an alarm wailed.

Garmen gave Adair a glare and hit the table's built-in intercom. "Garmen. What is wrong?"

"Jump wave detected!" Priam yelled.

"Distance?"

"Twenty hours ahead of us!"

"I am on my way up," Garmen said.

When he arrived on the bridge, Garmen headed for the holotable, followed by Satinka, Niyol, and Quartus. Niyol accessed the data, and the holotable lit up with the image of the outer planetary system. The *McKenna's Pride* was in the center, with the pursuing ships trailing after them and an area of pulsating space in front of them, indicating the emergence wave.

"Incoming ship!" Priam yelled. After a few seconds, a ship icon replaced the pulsating space.

"We need to ID that ship!" Garmen called out.

"That will take a few minutes!"

"Sensors! How long until they intercept us?"

"Assuming a 1.5 G burn and current courses, ten hours, sir!"

"I expect them to come in a lot faster than that," Quartus said. "Minimum of two Gs, if not more."

"Helm!" Satinka yelled. "Change course to ninety by sixty-five by one hundred! Increase thrust to 1.9 G! Cassie! How long to fast-charge the jump drive?"

"Ten hours!"

"Risk?"

"Considerable," Quartus replied. "There's a good chance we could destroy or damage the drive."

Garmen nodded, then looked at Satinka. "We have no choice. Fast-charge the drive."

"Cassie!" Satinka yelled. "Start fast-charging the drive!"

"*Aff*, Captain!"

"What about the jump coordinates?" Garmen asked.

Satinka exhaled. "They'll have to be reworked."

"How long?"

"A few hours, assuming we don't change course again."

"Sir!" Priam called out. "The ship has been identified! It is the *Lei Kung*!"

Niyol punched up the data and brought it up on the holotable. "*McKenna*-class, Goliath Scorpion."

"We seem to be awash in *McKenna*s all of a sudden," Satinka said sarcastically.

"Sir!" Priam called out again. "The *Lei Kung* is launching fighters and has already accelerated to 0.75 Gs!"

"Just what we needed." Garmen stared at the map. "Satinka, get that course figured out, *now*!"

CHAPTER 47

MCKENNA-CLASS WARSHIP SLS MCKENNA'S PRIDE
STRANA MECHTY SYSTEM
CLAN HOMEWORLDS
10 APRIL 3076
(JUMP DRIVE RECHARGE TIME REMAINING: 0 MINUTES)

The bridge was the quietest Garmen had seen since their arrival. He was standing at the holotable. Adair, Niyol, and Quartus were already there, staring at the images displayed over the table. Satinka paced the bridge like a caged smoke jaguar. The jump drive was charged, the jump coordinates entered into the computer. Now all they could do now is wait.

"Fifteen minutes to the proximity point," Niyol said.

Garmen stared at the holotable. The *Absolute Truth* was ten hours behind them, still pursuing, but losing ground. The *Sovereign Right* was three hours off their port stern, closing the distance steadily.

But the *Lei Kung* was the major concern now. The battleship was on an intercept course and closing fast.

"How long until the *Lei Kung* is in range?" he asked.

"Eight minutes until their aerofighters are in range," Niyol replied, his face haggard. They were pushing over two Gs now, and it was hard on everyone. "The DropShips are three minutes behind them, and the *Lei Kung* will be within firing range in thirteen minutes, but it is still accelerating."

"Sir!" Priam called out. "The *Truth*'s pursuing fighters are closing the distance, and their DropShips are right behind them! Also, the *Sovereign Right* has increased to 2.3 Gs and the *Absolute Truth* has increased to 1.9 Gs!"

Garmen glanced in Satinka's direction. She saw him and gave a tight smile.

"Captain!" Priam shouted, his voice hoarse from overuse. "The *Lei Kung* has altered course!"

Garmen spun back to the holotable. "Show me."

Niyol tapped a few buttons, and a line appeared showing the enemy battleship's new course. Garmen frowned as he saw it pass in front of the *Pride*'s current heading.

"They're planning to cross the *T*," Quartus said. He looked pale and was holding onto the table. "Put an entire broadside into our bow."

Garmen looked at him. "Can we alter course?"

Quartus shook his head. "If we do, it will throw off Satinka's jump calculations."

A burst of frustration flashed through Garmen. Before he could say anything, he felt a hand on his arm. He turned to glare at Quartus's calm, though strained, expression.

"We're doing the best we can," the merchant said. "And considering what we've done so far, we've done pretty well. Now is not the time to let your emotions get the best of you. We still have a chance, a better one than when we started. We'll see it through, Star Captain, for all of us."

Garmen inhaled a large breath, then exhaled. "Satinka! How long until we reach the proximity point?"

"Fourteen minutes, fifteen seconds!"

"Set the jump countdown clock for fourteen minutes, then alert the entire ship. I want every gunnery station manned and everyone else belted into a chair or a bunk. Tell them to be ready for combat."

"*Aff*, Star Captain!" Satinka sounded too cheerful for the situation. She tapped a few buttons on the nav console, and Garmen noticed several small panels around the bridge light up with 14:00:00. She moved over to the comms station and began pushing buttons there as well.

"Helm!" Garmen barked. "Hold this course and speed, no matter what happens!"

"*Aff*, sir!"

A shrill beep sounded throughout the ship, followed by Satinka's voice over the intercom. "Attention all crew and passengers! We jump in fourteen minutes, and it looks like we'll have to fight our way out! All Knives to your gunnery stations! Everyone else, strap in and hold on!"

The countdown timer started. Garmen watched it slowly tick off one second at a time. At ten minutes and thirty seconds, he turned the holotable off and moved to the captain's chair, where he could see another countdown clock on the wall at the front of the bridge. "All stations, check in."

As he sat, he heard the different sections check in. He strapped into the chair's restraint harness, then swung around to make sure everyone had done the same. Satinka was in the comms chair, Niyol at the damage-control station, while Adair and Quartus had chosen jump seats at the rear of the bridge.

The alarm stopped, and the silence was oppressive.

At eight minutes, Garmen said, "Cassandra, activate the jump alarm again."

The low siren pulsed through the ship once more.

Garmen adjusted the harness and tried to relax. "Stand by."

"Fighters coming in from astern, port astern, and port forward!" Priam's voice was rapid and higher pitched than normal. "DropShips are coming in behind them!"

"Weapons!" Satinka said into the intercom. "Missile teams, concentrate on the fighters! Main weapons, target the DropShips! Keep them off us! Helm! Hold steady!"

"H-holding!" Fayette shouted.

Garmen felt and heard the *Pride*'s weapons firing, the sound muffled by the numerous bulkheads between the bridge and the weapon stations. He looked up at the countdown timer. The numbers showed seven minutes, forty seconds, but it seemed like the timer was slowing down.

"Fighters are closing!" Priam shouted, his body visibly shaking with fear.

"Priam!" Satinka shouted, making Garmen look at her. "How long until the *Lei Kung* is in firing range?"

"Seven minutes, thirty seconds!"

Garmen glanced back at the countdown clock and saw the time pass the seven-minute, thirty-second mark. He felt helpless, stuck in this chair and unable to do anything to affect the battle raging around him. He had never felt this sensation before, and it made him furious.

"Fighters are opening fire!"

He could hear the faint explosions as the fighters' weapons ripped into the *Pride*'s thick armor. They would not hit anything vital on the first pass, but multiple passes and the DropShips' fire would weaken the armor just in time for the *Lei Kung* to follow up with its WarShip-killing weapons. He looked up at the timer just as it passed the seven-minute mark.

A louder explosion startled Garmen.

"Yago!" Satinka shouted. "What the hell was that?"

Yago scanned several different screens, his fingers moving rapidly across the control panel. "Stern naval laser two is offline! Compartment five-one-two has been breached!"

"Seal compartments five-one-one and five-one-three!"

Again, Yago's fingers flew across the control panel. "Compartments sealed! No further damage!"

"Captain!" Bran shouted. "Stern missile launchers report they have only three White Sharks and two Killer Whales left! No more Barracudas!"

"Tell them to pick their targets and hold their fire until they have a solid lock!" Satinka yelled. "Yago, how does our armor look?"

"Down between five and twenty percent! Heaviest damage is to the stern!"

Garmen's hands curled around the arms of the captain's chair. He should be doing something! He looked up at the timer and saw that only another thirty seconds had passed—still six and a half minutes until they could jump.

"DropShip off the starboard stern!" Priam shouted, making Garmen turn to look at him. The tech stared at the screen for several seconds, then his voice became a screech. "Great Father! It's a *Sassanid*-class troop carrier!"

Garmen's stomach clenched. *Sassanid*s could carry a full Trinary of Elementals—seventy-five troopers. Even without battle armor, that many troops could overwhelm his spread-out forces with ease.

"Bran! Focus every weapon you can on that *Sassanid*!" Satinka snarled. "Priam! Is it heading for a docking collar?"

"Er...*aff*! Dorsal collar, astern!"

"Cronan! Stand by to rotate the *Pride* ninety degrees to port!"

"What?" Garmen said, his throat dry. "Is that going to make our jump harder?"

She grinned at him. "Old merchant trick. They're trying to use a docking collar, and I plan to let them eat weapons fire instead. As for the jump, it won't matter what our orientation is. As long as we maintain the same speed and heading, we'll be able to jump. Priam! Keep tracking that *Sassanid*!"

"Fighters coming in from the forward starboard!"

"Never mind them! Keep tracking that *Sassanid*! If it docks with us, we'll be breathing vacuum quicker than you can blink!"

"Rear missile launchers report no more missiles!" Bran shouted.

"Then get them to other weapon stations! What's the status of the forward missile launchers?"

"Nine missiles left! Two each of the Killer Whales and White Sharks and five Barracudas!"

"Reserve the White Sharks and Killer Whales, and only use the Barracudas! Sensors! What's that *Sassanid* doing?"

"It's closing! Coming in fast!"

"Helm, rotate the *Pride* ninety degrees port! All starboard gunners, target the *Sassanid* and blow it to hell!"

Garmen could not feel the *Pride* roll, but he did hear the weapons firing.

A few seconds later the sensor tech shouted, "*Sassanid* is slowing and drifting! It's losing thrust!"

"We dodged a smoke jaguar there," Satinka said. "Priam, keep an eye out for any more *Sassanid*s! What about the *Lei Kung*?"

"Five and a half minutes to weapons range!"

Garmen looked up at the timer. It had dipped under six minutes, but there was still too much time.

"We're through the *Lei Kung*'s fighters and DropShip screen!" Priam yelled.

"It's going to take them a few minutes to turn around and come after us," Satinka said. "Bran, do the forward launchers have any missiles left?"

"Just the Killer Whales and White Sharks."

"Tell them to load all the remaining missiles and fire them along the *Lei Kung*'s projected course."

"Are we in range?" Garmen asked.

She grinned at him. "We are, but as fast as the *Lei Kung* is moving, it won't be able to perform evasive maneuvers. And those missiles will keep coming at them, even after their motors shut off. The crew will be more worried about them than us, just long enough for us to make the jump."

"You hope."

She shrugged. "We've been living on hope since we started this crazy plan. Why not one more thing to hope about?"

Garmen looked at the timer: five minutes and forty-five seconds left. He sighed. "Do what you have to."

"Missiles away!"

"Gunners!" Satinka said. "Concentrate on the DropShips! Ignore the fighters for now!"

"DropShip coming on an attack run from port stern!"

"Cronan! Rotate ninety degrees starboard! All portside weapons not already engaged, fire at that DropShip!"

"Compartments seven-one-two through seven-one-four are losing atmosphere!"

"Seal compartments seven-one-one through seven-one-five!"

"Sealing! I have a fire alarm in Cargo Hold Six!"

"Seal and purge!"

"*Aff*, Captain!"

Garmen sat and listened as the battle continued, feeling out of his depth and useless. The *McKenna's Pride* was fending off several Stars of fighters and half a dozen DropShips, and the *Lei Kung* neared with each passing second. The *Pride* was taking hit after hit, but it kept moving forward. Time slowed to a crawl as the battle happened around him, the lower-caste crew doing what he and his warriors should have been doing— fighting to save their lives.

When he finally glanced up, he stiffened: the timer had dropped to under a minute remaining. "Satinka!" he shouted. "Fifty-nine seconds!"

"I see!" She swung back to the comm panel and activated the intercom. "Attention, all crew and passengers! Less than one minute to jump! If you're not buckled in, do it now! Systems, seal all compartments! Gunners, do not let up! Engineering, stand by on the jump drive! Good luck, everyone!"

She turned the chair back to Garmen. "The command is yours. Jump us out of this."

He nodded, his gaze glued to the timer, only to hear Priam shout: "The *Lei Kung* has opened fire!"

Garmen gripped the arms of his chair, waiting for the impact. A couple seconds later, he heard Priam shout, "Our missiles hit! One, two, three hits!" Two seconds later, "Missile launch from the *Lei Kung*! Impact in twenty seconds!"

"How many?" Satinka demanded.

"Four Killer Whales!"

Garmen glanced up at the timer, showing more than thirty seconds remaining before they could jump. "Armor status on the bow?"

"More than ninety percent!"

"Fayette, hold your bearing and speed!" Satinka shouted. "How long before the *Lei Kung* is in position to fire that broadside?"

"Twenty-five seconds!"

Garmen glanced up just as the timer passed twenty-five seconds. "Jump on my command!" he said.

"You heard him!' Satinka shouted. "He's in charge!"

The timer dropped to twenty seconds, then fifteen.

"Missile impact in five seconds!" Priam shouted.

Three hard explosions shook the bridge, but Garmen's eyes never left the timer as it reached ten seconds...

Nine...

Eight...

"The *Lei Kung* has opened fire!" Priam shouted.

Five...

Four...

More explosions rattled the ship from somewhere forward, and Garmen glanced to Yago's station to see more red lights flash on his board. He glanced back at the timer in time to see the last seconds drop away...

Two...

One...

"Jump!"

The bridge around Garmen suddenly distorted as the *McKenna's Pride* tore a hole through hyperspace.

CHAPTER 48

Garmen found himself floating in cold, featureless black space. He looked around, but saw nothing. He tried to call out, but there was no sound. Had the jump failed? Had the *Lei Kung*'s broadside punched through the armor and depressurized the bridge? Were they all dead?

"You have failed!" a voice echoed. He looked around for a source, but there was none.

"A simple mission!" the voice said again, clear enough for Garmen to recognize it as Khan Vlad Ward. *"Five years to plan and prepare, and you still failed!"*

He spun around, but there was nothing to see.

The Khan's voice grew louder. *"If you were not already dead, I would have you executed!"*

A speck of light appeared in the darkness and suddenly grew, a bright white light that filled his entire vision—

The world came back together, and Garmen blinked rapidly as his brain tried to unscramble itself. He was on the *Pride*'s bridge, still strapped in the captain's chair. He looked around, ignoring the aching of his body. Everyone else was moving, though several of them grimaced in pain.

"Status report?" he managed to say.

"That went much smoother than I expected." Quartus grimaced. "Though I'm not sure all my organs are still in the right spots."

"Damage control," Niyol said, his tone hushed as he looked over his board. "The jump overloaded several system panels, but they should be easy to fix."

"Major systems report green across the board."

"Sensors are picking up no ships within range.

"We made it," Satinka said in a hushed tone, then louder, "We made it!"

Shouts of joy filled the bridge, and Garmen noticed even the dour Adair grinning. He felt his own joy, but it was tempered by knowledge they had a long way to go.

"Celebrate later," he said. "I want a visual check of all compartments, and a full damage assessment. Get those overloaded panels looked at."

Satinka nodded and moved to look at the navigator's screen. "Looks like we're in the right place. Helm, if the engines are online, get us underway and head for the zenith point. Point-nine Gs for now."

"*Aff*, Captain."

"Quartus, you able to move?"

"Right now, my dear, I could dance!"

"Dance later. I need you to get on comms and let the rest of the fleet know it's us and not the Grand Council come to get them."

"Of course. That emergence wave will show up on their sensors like a supernova, and I have no doubt a few people have already started pulling in their jump sails and preparing to run." He stood slowly, his feet leaving the deck for a few seconds before he slowly came down. "It'll take me a couple of minutes to adjust to normal gravity."

Satinka nodded. "While you're at it, let the rest of the crew know we made it." She looked around the bridge. "Good job, people, but we're not out of the woods yet."

For several minutes, there was quiet chatter as different posts reported in and the crew shook off post-jump shock. Quartus made the announcement that they had made the jump successfully, then started composing a message for the fleet.

Garmen unbuckled his harness and stood on shaky legs. "Start sensor sweep and send the results to the holotable."

He trudged to the back of the bridge, where Satinka, Niyol, and Quartus soon joined him. He activated the holotable, which displayed a planetary system, one with a bright star in the center, surrounded by several gas giants and small rocky planets.

"Welcome to Nowhere," Quartus said. "Best known as Star System H-2543 in the Clan navigational directory. We are twenty-seven light-years from Strana Mechty and fifteen from Ironhold."

Garmen nodded. "Time to zenith point?"

"As current speed, seven hours," Satinka replied.

"Why this system?" Garmen asked.

"Besides being uninhabited?" Satinka zoomed in on the star. "A B-nine main sequence star. Drive recharge time is only one hundred and sixty hours, which means once we reach the zenith point, we can use our jump sail to charge the drive much quicker than we would normally." She zoomed out again to display a number of icons clustered at the zenith point. "The rest of our people. I didn't want to risk a collision by jumping in on top of them." She looked at Quartus. "Message sent?"

The merchant nodded. "I included some personal messages, to let them know it's us. We should be getting a reply within the hour."

Garmen nodded. "We have made a good start, but we are not out of Clan Space yet." He thought he saw a flicker of disappointment on Satinka's face, but ignored it. "No doubt they will be looking for us."

"There are three hundred and twenty-seven stars within a thirty-light-year radius of Strana Mechty," Satinka said. "It'll take time to search them all."

Quartus nodded. "That's why Satinka and I decided to use A-, B-, and F-class stars for our first five jumps. By our sixth jump, they'll never be able to find us."

"Once we rendezvous with the rest of the fleet, we can skim a few pilots and engineers from the other vessels, to give the *Pride* a real crew," Satinka added.

"Good," Garmen said. "We can also check the *Pride* from bow to stern for any problems." He smiled at them. "This is the first step in a long journey. Let us make sure we are ready for the next step."

Five hours later, Garmen stared at the holotable in disbelief. "What? How is this possible?"

The holotable image showed a large number of JumpShips waiting for them at the zenith point. He had expected six or seven, but eighteen JumpShips, ranging from a pair of *Monolith*s and an *Odyssey* all the way down to a single *Hunter*-class JumpShip, were sitting with jump sails unfurled. A side graph listed forty DropShips attached to the JumpShips. Only he and Satinka were at the holotable, as most of the crew, including Niyol and Quartus, were getting some much-needed rest.

The *Pride* had taken damage, but was still mobile and jump capable. A number of compartments had been sealed off due to damage, and no one had gone outside to inspect the hull, but there were no major problems.

"A few of my captains knew a few other unhappy captains and sounded them out," Satinka said with a grin, then motioned to the image. "You see the result."

"How many people?" he asked.

"According to the *Gray Mist*'s message, there's between eighteen hundred to twenty-two hundred civilians. They're still counting and should have a solid number by the time we reach them."

Garmen looked at her in shock. "Do we have enough supplies?"

"We'll check, but I think we'll be all right."

He nodded, still stunned by the number of people taking a chance to leave Clan Space with them. "How long to reach the fleet?"

"Two hours."

"Good. Anything else?"

Satinka's smile turned predatory. "I do have an... experiment I want to try when we get to the jump point," she purred, walking around the holotable.

He felt like he was being stalked by a smoke jaguar. "What?"

She put her arms around her neck. "What do you think coupling is like in zero G?"

CHAPTER 49

CENTRAL SECTOR
KATYUSHA CITY
STRANA MECHTY
CLAN HOMEWORLDS
10 APRIL 3076

"They have jumped." Kyne sounded exhausted.

Telinov stared at him, his words not registering for several seconds. Mikino, on the other hand, understood right away.

"What do you mean they *jumped*?" he roared. "They jumped while moving?"

"*Aff*, Star Colonel," Kyne replied. "It is risky to do, but it is possible."

Mikino exhaled slowly. "I will inform the ilKhan."

Telinov roused from her first real sleep in the last several days. She reluctantly opened her eyes to see Sergis standing over her, shaking her awake.

"The ilKhan is here," he said, "and he wishes to speak to both the Ebon and Katyusha Keshik commanders."

She groaned and sat up. The break room had a couch, and she had used her rank to claim it. She yawned and sat up. "How long was I out?"

"About three hours."

She groaned again. "I would kill for some coffee."

"No need." Steiner handed her a steaming cup. "The meeting starts in five minutes."

By the time she entered the conference room, the ilKhan was already there, along with Mikino, Steiner, and Kyne on the one side, while the senior Katyusha Keshik leadership—Star Colonel Savill Truscott, Star Captain Ingria Raiz, and Star Commander Brunhild Mannix—mirrored the Ebon Keshik representatives.

Telinov could feel the tension as she took the empty seat between Mikino and Steiner. Raiz's arm was in a sling, and the left side of her face was a mass of bruises, while the other two Katyusha officers looked disheveled and depleted.

As soon as Telinov sat down, ilKhan Hannibal Banacek looked from one set of commanders to the other. "We have much to do, so you will sit and listen," he said, an undercurrent of anger in his voice. "You are all at fault. None of you uncovered this... desecration, so you are all equally at fault. I should send all of you back to your Clans in disgrace."

He inhaled deeply. "But...I am not going to. Instead, we are going to publicly claim that the 'Mech attack was carried out by members of the Society attempting to destroy the Master Genetic Repository, while a few of their cohorts used the confusion to steal the *McKenna's Pride* and flee into the unknown. Privately, all of you *will* find whoever did this. I want every single person even remotely involved with this incident arrested and interrogated. I do not care what you have to do, but I want them *found*! Understood?"

"*Aff, ilKhan!*" the seven shouted.

"Star Colonel Truscott, you and your people can leave. You have sweeps to conduct, *quiaff*?"

"*Aff*, ilKhan," Truscott replied quietly.

The three Katyusha members rose and left.

After the door closed behind them, Banacek looked at the four Ebon Keshik members. "I am still angry at you, but you did better than most would have, all things considered. And I understand Warrior Kyne has suggested a plan to salvage something from this fiasco, *quiaff*?"

Telinov glanced down the table at the analyst, who lowered his eyes. "It was just a thought spoken out loud, ilKhan. I did not know you were there."

"But it is worth pursuing. The loss of the Great Father's body and *McKenna's Pride* is a deep blow that could fracture the Grand Council and jeopardize our traditions, our way of life. Therefore, in three days, I am going to announce that we have found the Great Father's body floating in space near where the *Pride* jumped."

"But—" Telinov said.

"You will go out and 'find' the body and bring it back to Strana Mechty. At the same time I announce the recovery of the Great Father's body, I will order a tomb built adjacent to the Hall of Khans, and the Great Father's body will be interred under a multi-ton block of granite, visible through the glass sides."

"But the Grand Council will demand a DNA test to ensure it is the Great Father," Steiner said.

Banacek nodded. "They will, but floating in space without protection from cosmic radiation does things to one's DNA. It will not be difficult to switch all known samples with samples from the imposter."

"Imposter?" Mikino asked.

Banacek nodded. "Stas, the commander of these so-called Wraiths who attacked this headquarters, looks enough like the Great Father to withstand a cursory glance, and by the time a medical team finishes with the body, it will be difficult to tell them apart. Also, according to this former warrior's codex, he is a descendant of the Great Father through Nicholas, so his DNA will be easier to manipulate."

"The Grand Council—"

"Even if they are suspicious, they realize that the Great Father is a symbol we must have. A fractured Council is the last thing we need, so they will swallow their suspicions. After a few generations, it will no longer matter."

He gave them a cold look. "Besides the three crew members on the DropShip that 'discover' the body and the three scientists who alter and preserve it, we in this room are the only ones who will know about this. Say one word about this, to anyone, and you will disappear, your entire existence scrubbed from your Clan's records as if you never existed. And I *will* know. Am I clear?"

"*Aff*," Mikino replied. "And we will keep silent, because you are right. We need Unity now, and the Great Father's tomb can provide it."

"Good. The body will be released to you tomorrow. Star Captain Telinov, you will leave the day after tomorrow on my DropShip, the *Serpent's Fang*. You will search the area of space near the jump point and make a big deal about finding the body. Is that clear?"

"*Aff*, ilKhan."

"That is all. Do not discuss this outside of this room. The rumors will be bad enough without adding to them." Banacek rose and strode out of the room.

After the door closed behind the ilKhan, Mikino rose and looked at the other three. "We will follow the ilKhan's orders."

"But is that a good idea?" Telinov slumped into her chair, feeling even more tired.

"Remember what I told you when you reported to me on your first day?" Mikino said.

Telinov shook her head. "*Neg*, sir."

"We handle problems that threaten our society before they can rise to the Grand Council's attention. This is one of those problems."

"*Aff*, sir."

"Star Colonel?" Steiner said. "The Star Captain is short on sleep and not thinking clearly. I suggest we discuss this in the morning, once we have all gotten some badly needed rest."

The Elemental nodded. "That is a good idea. I am also uncomfortable with this plan, but it has been left to us to execute, and we will do so. Get some sleep, Bhu. We have a full day in front of us." He walked out, leaving the three of them.

"Kyne?" Steiner said.

"Yes, Star Commander?"

"Go get some sleep. We have a lot to do with hunting the people behind this down, and I want you fresh and ready."

Kyne nodded once. "*Aff*, sir."

Steiner sighed. "But first," Telinov heard him say as she drifted off to sleep, "help me carry the Star Captain to one of the guest quarters..."

CHAPTER 50

Wolf Khan Vlad Ward's first words to Garmen were, "I told you to reclaim the body, not steal the entire *stravag* ship!"

Garmen was not sure if the Khan was angry, impressed, or amused, so he stayed at attention.

They were standing in one of the *Pride*'s small-craft bays. The Khan had used a shuttle to get from his *Star Lord* to the battleship. Vlad, along with a couple of aides, had floated out of the shuttle and used magnetic boots to anchor themselves to the deck.

"It was not by choice, my Khan," Garmen said. Behind him, three of his Points and Niyol's Point stood at attention, the only people in the hangar. "But it became necessary once the original plan was compromised." He presented Vlad a memory crystal. "My full report."

Ward took it and nodded. "This will make an interesting read." He put it into a pocket, then said, "I take it you had significant trouble in your mission?"

"*Aff*, my Khan. I do not know how much you know of the situation in Clan Space, but Star Commander Niyol has compiled a detailed report of the last five years." Garmen presented a set of memory crystals.

Vlad pocketed them. "I want to see the Great Father."

"Of course. This way."

CRAIG A. REED, JR.

They floated through the corridors until they reached the tomb. Garmen's Point had the duty shift, guarding the body. Vlad activated his boots' magnetic soles and stood next to the body. "You did well, Star Captain, even if it did take years."

"Thank you, my Khan."

"I take it you had help?"

"I did what I had to do." His report did not mention the JumpShip fleet that had come with them, and it also downplayed Satinka and her people's roles. There were a few things the Khan did not need to know.

Like Garmen and Satinka's son.

Somewhere in the last six years, Garmen's birth control implant had failed, while Satinka's had been reversed upon her ejection from the warrior caste. Andery had been born three months ago, and both had agreed the name was right. He was with his mother now, safely out of the Khan's reach. He did not know whether he would ever see them again, but the fact both lived was good enough for now.

As for Satinka's people, some had moved into the Lyran Alliance, but others, including Satinka, had decided to see more of what the Inner Sphere had to offer. This meant the *Pride* had been alone when Vlad's two ships jumped into the system.

Vlad placed a hand on the ferroglass covering the general's coffin. "How much do you know about current events in the Inner Sphere?"

"Very little, my Khan. We know there is fighting everywhere. The genetic leg—"

"They are all safe," Vlad interrupted, "even Nicholas and Andery's."

Garmen felt a measure of relief wash over him. "Our reports include details on the Kopis raid and the aftermath. The results were much worse than you would expect."

"I see. Regardless, as much as I want to announce we have the Great Father's body, to do so now would make it an instant target for the other Clans and the Word of Blake. It will be hidden until the time the Wolves can move to claim Terra."

He looked back at Garmen. "But what am I to do with you and your Star? You have been gone for six years. Too many questions will be asked, too many suspicions will be aroused at your sudden reappearance."

Dread gripped Garmen. "My Khan?"

"You have done the Clan a great service, Star Captain. By rights, you should be lauded for what you have done. But I cannot reinstate your Star in the Wolves at this time."

The dread deepened into fear. "What will you do with us?"

"Have you heard of Devlin Stone?"

"We have heard rumors."

"Stone has created and leads a coalition of Clan and Inner Sphere forces in the fight against the Word of Blake. He could use a warrior like you. The Trinary I am sending Stone is in need of a Star Captain to lead it, and that command is now yours. Niyol's Point will accompany you to handle intelligence matters. You will show everyone—Word of Blake, the Spheroids, and the other Clans—that Wolves are still the dominant warriors."

Confusion, bitterness, and disappointment welled up inside Garmen, but he kept it from showing on his face. "*Aff*, my Khan!"

"Good. A DropShip is bringing a skeleton crew for the *Pride*. You and your Star will board it and dock with the *Black Howl*, which will take you to your new command. You will speak to no one about this matter. As far as Devlin Stone and your new command will know, your Star was on a deep-penetration raid outside our occupation zone, and has recently returned."

"Understood."

"Now, I wish to be alone with the Great Father."

"*Aff*, my Khan."

Garmen and all but one of Vlad's aides floated out of the room. As soon as the hatch closed, the aide, a blond woman, smiled. "It took them long enough."

"But they succeeded."

Katherine Wolf, formerly Katherine Morgan Steiner-Davion, looked toward the hatch. "He could be a threat to you."

"He is not." Vlad took his hand off the ferroglass and turned off the boots so he could float. "He has Warden views, plus he has no power base within the Clan—being away for six years has not helped. And we both know Stone does not shy away from a fight—so there is a good chance Garmen will not survive anyway."

"If he mentions anything about—"

"You do not know him." Vlad floated over to the window. "I told him the truth. If the presence of this ship and Great Father's body became known, people would search for it, either to take it for their own or destroy it. Trust me, he will stay silent."

"You sound so sure."

Vlad smiled. "I am."

"What are you going to do with this ship?"

"Oh, I already know where to hide it, but you will return to the *Black Howl* and accompany Garmen Kerensky as far as Tamar. The rest of us will take the *McKenna's Pride* and hide it until the time is right to reveal it."

She barked a laugh. "You do not trust me."

"When it comes to this, there are few I trust. Even the ships' crews will not know where we are hiding it. I have a list of jump coordinates and will input them myself."

She raised an eyebrow. "All this trouble for a body?"

"Not just a body—the Great Father himself. Nicholas created the Clans though force of will, but it was the Great Father who gave us our purpose. One day he will return to Terra, and on that day he will see what we have reclaimed."

EPILOGUE

SYSTEM M-2343
DARK NEBULA
CLAN HELL'S HORSES OCCUPATION ZONE
19 JULY 3147
(70 YEARS LATER)

A good place to hide a precious treasure, saKhan Garner Kerensky thought as the airlock cycled. Like the others in the airlock, he was wearing a full spacesuit, as the first Elementals on board had indicated the *Pride*'s life support was offline. *In orbit around a gas giant's moon in a backwater system inside a nebula. Khan Ward was either a genius or insane.*

The airlock finished its cycle and the door slid open, revealing a dimly lit corridor. Two Elementals from the Point assigned to escort him floated through the hatch and took up positions flanking it. Garner came through next, and he pushed off to one side as his aide and the rest of his security Point followed him out of the airlock.

"Kerensky to all boarding Points. Status?"

"Point Two-Three. Bridge secured."

"Point Two-Four. Engine room secured."

"Point Two-Five. Auxiliary control secured."

"Point Two-One. We have secured the tomb and the Great Father's body."

"Point Two-Two. Crew quarters are still being swept."

Garner turned to the Elemental Star Commander. "Get the rest of your Star on board. Once we have the ship fully secured, get the techs to bring life support online, and I want a full report on the ship's status in six hours."

"*Aff*, saKhan!"

"In the meantime, I want to see the Great Father's body."

Garner stared down at the man who was his ancestor. "So, it is true," he muttered.

"How did he get here?" Star Captain Neil whispered over the radio.

Only three of them were in the room—Garner, his aide Neil, and Point Commander Carson, the security leader. All three were from Kerensky bloodlines, making it easy for Garner to decide who should see the body first.

Garner turned to Neil. "I do not know, and we will probably never know. That secret died with Khan Vlad Ward."

"What was he thinking?" Carson asked, gazing down at the Great Father.

Garner shrugged. "All the evidence indicates that only Vlad and a few close aides knew about this ship's whereabouts, and only Vlad himself knew where it was hidden."

Garner's radio chirped. "Jafar here," the *Pride*'s new captain said. "We have checked the life support, and it should be up within the half-hour."

"Anything else I should know?" Garner asked.

"It is clear the *Pride* was in a serious battle at some time in the past. Several sealed compartment read as being open to vacuum, and the armor damage is widespread."

"Will that be a problem?"

"*Neg*, I do not think so. We are checking the cargo holds for spare parts and replacement armor. Otherwise, the *Boarhound* has enough supplies to finish the repairs. I do want to fully investigate the engines before we attempt to move it, just to be safe."

"Do so. Prioritize all systems we need to move the *Pride* out of this system."

"*Aff*, saKhan. When can I expect the rest of the crew to arrive?"

"Six hours. Kerensky out." He changed channels on his radio. "Kerensky to *Cold Fang*. Deploy your fighters. I want two Stars on CAP, and the third in reserve."

"*Aff*, saKhan."

Through the tomb's viewport, Garner could see the *Odyssey* JumpShip he had arrived on, one of two assigned to this mission and manned by Wolf Watch crews. "Kerensky to *Silent Hunter*. Contact the *Shadow Wolf* and order it to join us."

The one hundred officers and crew currently on board would soon be joined by a hundred and fifty more, giving the *Pride* enough crew to get it and the Great Father into Wolf Empire territory—and, when the time was right, to Terra.

He looked down at General Kerensky's body. *I wonder what you would say when we bring you home after so long?* he thought. *I wonder how you got here to begin with. That must be an event worthy of* The Remembrance.

Garner shook his head. Idle thoughts for a later time. "Star Captain, get the honor guard in here now."

BATTLETECH GLOSSARY

Clan military unit designations are used throughout this book:

Point: 1 'Mech or 5 infantry
Star: 5 'Mechs or 25 infantry
Binary: 2 Stars
Trinary: 3 Stars
Cluster: 4–5 Binaries/Trinaries
Galaxy: 3-5 Clusters
Nova: 1 'Mech Star and 1 infantry Star
Supernova: 1 'Mech Binary and 2 infantry Stars

ABTAKHA

An *abtakha* is a captured warrior who is adopted into his new Clan as a warrior.

AUTOCANNON

This is a rapid-fire, auto-loading weapon. Light autocannons range from 30 to 90 millimeter (mm), and heavy autocannons may be from 80 to 120mm or more. They fire high-speed streams of high-explosive, armor-piercing shells.

BATCHALL

The *batchall* is the ritual by which Clan warriors issue combat challenges. Though the type of challenge varies, most begin with the challenger identifying themselves, stating the prize of the contest, and requesting that the defender identify the forces at their disposal. The defender also has the right to name the location of the trial. The two sides then bid for what forces will participate in the contest. The subcommander who bids to fight with the number of forces wins the right and responsibility to make the attack. The defender may increase the stakes by demanding a prize of equal or lesser value if they wish.

BATTLEMECH

BattleMechs are the most powerful war machines ever built. First developed by Terran scientists and engineers, these huge vehicles are faster, more mobile, better-armored and more heavily armed than any twentieth-century tank. Ten to twelve meters tall and equipped with particle projection cannons, lasers, rapid-fire autocannon and missiles, they pack enough firepower to flatten anything but another BattleMech. A small fusion reactor provides virtually unlimited power, and BattleMechs can be adapted to fight in environments ranging from sun-baked deserts to subzero arctic icefields.

BLOODNAME

A Bloodname is the surname associated with a Bloodright, descended from one of the 800 warriors who stood with Nicholas Kerensky to form the Clans. A warrior must win the use of a Bloodname in a Trial of Bloodright. Only Bloodnamed warriors may sit on Clan Councils or hold the post of Loremaster, Khan, or ilKhan, and only the genetic material from the Bloodnamed is used in the warrior caste eugenics program.

BONDCORD

A woven bracelet worn by bondsmen who has been captured and claimed by a Clan member. Warrior-caste bondsmen wear a three-strand bondcord on their right wrists, with the color and patterning of the cords signifying the Clan and unit responsible for the warrior's capture. The cords represent integrity, fidelity, and prowess. The bondholder may cut each strand as he or she feels the bondsman demonstrates the associated quality. According to tradition, when the final cord is severed, the bondsman is considered a free member of his or her new Clan and adopted into the Warrior caste. Each Clan follows this tradition to varying degrees. For example, Clan Wolf accepts nearly all worthy individuals regardless of their past, while Clan Smoke Jaguar generally chose to adopt only trueborn warriors.

BONDSMAN

A bondsman is a prisoner held in a form of indentured servitude until released or accepted into the Clan. Most often, bondsmen are captured warriors who fulfill roles in the laborer or technician castes. Their status is represented by a woven bondcord, and they are obliged by honor and tradition to work for their captors to the best of their abilities.

CASTE

The Clans are divided into five castes: warrior, scientist, merchant, technician, and laborer, in descending order of influence. Each has many subcastes based on specialized skills. The warrior caste is largely the product of the artificial breeding program; those candidates who fail their Trial of Position are assigned to the scientist or technician caste, giving those castes a significant concentration of trueborn members. Most of the civilian castes are made up of the results of scientist-decreed arranged marriages within the castes.

The children of all castes undergo intensive scrutiny during their schooling to determine the caste for which they are best suited, though most end up in the same caste as their parents. This process allows children born to members of civilian castes to enter training to become warriors, though they belong to the less-prestigious ranks of the freeborn.

CIRCLE OF EQUALS

The area in which a trial takes place is known as the Circle of Equals. It ranges in size from a few dozen feet for personal combat to tens of miles for large-scale trials. Though traditionally a circle, the area can be any shape.

CRUSADER

A Crusader is a Clansman who espouses the invasion of the Inner Sphere and the re-establishment of the Star League by military force. Most Crusaders are contemptuous of the people of the Inner Sphere, whom they view as barbarians, and of freeborns within their own Clans.

DEZGRA

Any disgraced individual or unit is known as *dezgra*. Disgrace may come through refusing orders, failing in an assigned task, acting dishonorably, or demonstrating cowardice.

DROPSHIPS

Because interstellar JumpShips must avoid entering the heart of a solar system, they must "dock" in space at a considerable distance from a system's inhabited worlds. DropShips were developed for interplanetary travel. As the name implies, a DropShip is attached to hardpoints on the JumpShip's drive core, later to be dropped from the parent vessel after in-system entry. Though incapable of FTL travel, DropShips are highly maneuverable, well-armed and sufficiently aerodynamic to take off from and land on a planetary surface. The journey from the jump point to the inhabited worlds of a system usually requires a normal-space journey of several days or weeks, depending on the type of star.

FREEBIRTH

Freebirth is a Clan epithet used by trueborn members of the warrior caste to express disgust or frustration. For one trueborn to use this curse to refer to another trueborn is considered a mortal insult.

FREEBORN

An individual conceived and born by natural means is referred to as freeborn. Its emphasis on the artificial breeding program allows Clan society to view such individuals as second-class citizens.

HEGIRA

Hegira is the rite by which a defeated foe may withdraw from the field of battle without further combat and with no further loss of honor.

ISORLA

The spoils of battle, including bondsmen, claimed by the victorious warriors is called *isorla*.

JUMPSHIPS

Interstellar travel is accomplished via JumpShips, first developed in the twenty-second century. These somewhat ungainly vessels consist of a long, thin drive core and a sail resembling an enormous parasol, which can extend up to a kilometer in width. The ship is named for its ability to "jump" instantaneously across vast distances of space. After making its jump, the ship cannot travel until it has recharged by gathering up more solar energy.

The JumpShip's enormous sail is constructed from a special metal that absorbs vast quantities of electromagnetic energy from the nearest star. When it has soaked up enough energy, the sail transfers it to the drive core, which converts it into a space-twisting field. An instant later, the ship arrives at the next jump point, a distance of up to thirty light-years. This field is known as hyperspace, and its discovery opened to mankind the gateway to the stars.

JumpShips never land on planets. Interplanetary travel is carried out by DropShips, vessels that are attached to the JumpShip until arrival at the jump point.

KHAN (kaKhan, saKhan)

Each Clan Council elects two of its number as Khans, who serve as rulers of the Clan and its representatives on the Grand Council.

Traditionally, these individuals are the best warriors in the Clan, but in practice many Clans instead elect their most skilled politicians. The senior Khan, sometimes referred to as the kaKhan, acts as the head of the Clan, overseeing relationships between castes and Clans. The junior Khan, known as the saKhan, acts as the Clan's warlord. The senior Khan decides the exact distribution of tasks, and may assign the saKhan additional or different duties.

The term "kaKhan" is considered archaic, and is rarely used.

LASER

An acronym for "Light Amplification through Stimulated Emission of Radiation." When used as a weapon, the laser damages the target by concentrating extreme heat onto a small area. BattleMech lasers are designated as small, medium or large. Lasers are also available as shoulder-fired weapons operating from a portable backpack power unit. Certain range-finders and targeting equipment also employ low-level lasers.

LRM

This is an abbreviation for "Long-Range Missile," an indirect-fire missile with a high-explosive warhead.

POSSESSION, TRIAL OF

A Trial of Possession resolves disputes between two parties over ownership or control. This can include equipment, territory, or even genetic material. The traditional *batchall* forms the core of the trial in order to encourage the participants to resolve the dispute with minimal use of force.

REMEMBRANCE, THE

The Remembrance is an ongoing heroic saga that describes Clan history from the time of the Exodus to the present day. Each Clan maintains its own version, reflecting its opinions and perceptions of events. Inclusion in The Remembrance is one of the highest honors possible for a member of the Clans. All Clan warriors can recite passages from The Remembrance from memory, and written copies of the book are among the few nontechnical books allowed in Clan society. These books are usually lavishly illustrated in a fashion similar to the illuminated manuscripts and Bibles of the medieval period. Warriors frequently paint passages of The Remembrance on the sides of their OmniMechs, fighters, and battle armor.

SEYLA

Seyla is a ritual response in Clan ceremonies. The origin of this phrase is unknown, though it may come from the Biblical notation "selah," thought to be a musical notation or a reference to contemplation.

SRM

This is the abbreviation for "Short-Range Missile," a direct-trajectory missile with high-explosive or armor-piercing explosive warheads. They have a range of less than one kilometer and are only reliably accurate at ranges of less than 300 meters. They are more powerful, however, than LRMs.

SUCCESSOR LORDS

After the fall of the first Star League, the remaining members of the High Council each asserted his or her right to become First Lord. Their star empires became known as the Successor States and the rulers as Successor Lords. The Clan Invasion temporarily interrupted centuries of warfare known as the Succession Wars, which first began in 2786.

SURAT

A Clan epithet, alluding to the rodent of the same name, which disparages an individual's genetic heritage. As such, it is one of the most vulgar and offensive epithets among the Clans.

TOUMAN

The fighting arm of a Clan is known as the touman.

TROTHKIN

Used formally, trothkin refers to members of an extended sibko. It is more commonly used to denote members of a gathering, and warriors also frequently use it when addressing someone they consider a peer.

TRUEBORN/TRUEBIRTH

A warrior born of the Clan's artificial breeding program is known as a trueborn. In less formal situations, the Clans use the term truebirth.

WARDEN

A Warden is a Clansman who believes that the Clans were established to guard the Inner Sphere from outside threats rather than to conquer it and re-establish the Star League by force. Most Wardens were opposed to the recent invasion of the Inner Sphere.

ZELLBRIGEN

Zellbrigen is the body of rules governing duels. These rules dictate that such actions are one-on-one engagements, and that any warriors not immediately challenged should stay out of the battle until an opponent is free.

Once a Clan warrior engages a foe, no other warriors on his or her side may target that foe, even if it means allowing the death of the Clan warrior. Interfering in a duel by attacking a foe that is already engaged constitutes a major breach of honor, and usually results in loss of rank. Such action also opens the battle to a melee.

BATTLETECH ERAS

The *BattleTech* universe is a living, vibrant entity that grows each year as more sourcebooks and fiction are published. A dynamic universe, its setting and characters evolve over time within a highly detailed continuity framework, bringing everything to life in a way a static game universe cannot match.

To help quickly and easily convey the timeline of the universe—and to allow a player to easily "plug in" a given novel or sourcebook—we've divided *BattleTech* into six major eras.

STAR LEAGUE
(Present-2780)

Ian Cameron, ruler of the Terran Hegemony, concludes decades of tireless effort with the creation of the Star League, a political and military alliance between all Great Houses and the Hegemony. Star League armed forces immediately launch the Reunification War, forcing the Periphery realms to join. For the next two centuries, humanity experiences a golden age across the thousand light-years of human-occupied space known as the Inner Sphere. It also sees the creation of the most powerful military in human history.

(This era also covers the centuries before the founding of the Star League in 2571, most notably the Age of War.)

SUCCESSION WARS
(2781-3049)

Every last member of First Lord Richard Cameron's family is killed during a coup launched by Stefan Amaris. Following the thirteen-year war to unseat him, the rulers of each of the five Great Houses disband the Star League. General Aleksandr Kerensky departs with eighty percent of the Star League Defense Force beyond known space and the Inner Sphere collapses into centuries of warfare known as the Succession Wars that will eventually result in a massive loss of technology across most worlds.

CLAN INVASION
(3050-3061)

A mysterious invading force strikes the coreward region of the Inner Sphere. The invaders, called the Clans, are descendants of Kerensky's SLDF troops, forged into a society dedicated to becoming the greatest fighting force in history. With vastly superior technology and warriors, the Clans conquer world after world. Eventually this outside threat will forge a new Star League, something hundreds of years of warfare failed to accomplish. In addition, the Clans will act as a catalyst for a technological renaissance.

CIVIL WAR
(3062-3067)

The Clan threat is eventually lessened with the complete destruction of a Clan. With that massive external threat apparently neutralized, internal conflicts explode around the Inner Sphere. House Liao conquers its former Commonality, the St. Ives Compact; a rebellion of military units belonging to House Kurita sparks a war with their powerful border enemy, Clan Ghost Bear; the fabulously powerful Federated Commonwealth of House Steiner and House Davion collapses into five long years of bitter civil war.

JIHAD
(3067-3080)

Following the Federated Commonwealth Civil War, the leaders of the Great Houses meet and disband the new Star League, declaring it a sham. The pseudo-religious Word of Blake—a splinter group of ComStar, the protectors and controllers of interstellar communication—launch the Jihad: an interstellar war that pits every faction against each other and even against themselves, as weapons of mass destruction are used for the first time in centuries while new and frightening technologies are also unleashed.

DARK AGE
(3081-3150)

Under the guidance of Devlin Stone, the Republic of the Sphere is born at the heart of the Inner Sphere following the Jihad. One of the more extensive periods of peace begins to break out as the 32nd century dawns. The factions, to one degree or another, embrace disarmament, and the massive armies of the Succession Wars begin to fade. However, in 3132 eighty percent of interstellar communications collapses, throwing the universe into chaos. Wars erupt almost immediately, and the factions begin rebuilding their armies.

LOOKING FOR MORE HARD HITTING BATTLETECH FICTION?

WE'LL GET YOU RIGHT BACK INTO THE BATTLE!

Catalyst Game Labs brings you the very best in *BattleTech* fiction, available at most ebook retailers, including Amazon, Apple Books, Kobo, Barnes & Noble, and more!

NOVELS

1. *Decision at Thunder Rift* by William H. Keith Jr.
2. *Mercenary's Star* by William H. Keith Jr.
3. *The Price of Glory* by William H. Keith, Jr.
4. *Warrior: En Garde* by Michael A. Stackpole
5. *Warrior: Riposte* by Michael A. Stackpole
6. *Warrior: Coupé* by Michael A. Stackpole
7. *Wolves on the Border* by Robert N. Charrette
8. *Heir to the Dragon* by Robert N. Charrette
9. *Lethal Heritage* (The Blood of Kerensky, Volume 1) by Michael A. Stackpole
10. *Blood Legacy* (The Blood of Kerensky, Volume 2) by Michael A. Stackpole
11. *Lost Destiny* (The Blood of Kerensky, Volume 3) by Michael A. Stackpole
12. *Way of the Clans* (Legend of the Jade Phoenix, Volume 1) by Robert Thurston
13. *Bloodname* (Legend of the Jade Phoenix, Volume 2) by Robert Thurston
14. *Falcon Guard* (Legend of the Jade Phoenix, Volume 3) by Robert Thurston
15. *Wolf Pack* by Robert N. Charrette
16. *Main Event* by James D. Long
17. *Natural Selection* by Michael A. Stackpole
18. *Assumption of Risk* by Michael A. Stackpole
19. *Blood of Heroes* by Andrew Keith
20. *Close Quarters* by Victor Milán
21. *Far Country* by Peter L. Rice
22. *D.R.T.* by James D. Long
23. *Tactics of Duty* by William H. Keith
24. *Bred for War* by Michael A. Stackpole
25. *I Am Jade Falcon* by Robert Thurston
26. *Highlander Gambit* by Blaine Lee Pardoe
27. *Hearts of Chaos* by Victor Milán
28. *Operation Excalibur* by William H. Keith
29. *Malicious Intent* by Michael A. Stackpole
30. *Black Dragon* by Victor Milán
31. *Impetus of War* by Blaine Lee Pardoe
32. *Double-Blind* by Loren L. Coleman
33. *Binding Force* by Loren L. Coleman
34. *Exodus Road* (Twilight of the Clans, Volume 1) by Blaine Lee Pardoe
35. *Grave Covenant* ((Twilight of the Clans, Volume 2) by Michael A. Stackpole

36. *The Hunters* (Twilight of the Clans, Volume 3) by Thomas S. Gressman
37. *Freebirth* (Twilight of the Clans, Volume 4) by Robert Thurston
38. *Sword and Fire* (Twilight of the Clans, Volume 5) by Thomas S. Gressman
39. *Shadows of War* (Twilight of the Clans, Volume 6) by Thomas S. Gressman
40. *Prince of Havoc* (Twilight of the Clans, Volume 7) by Michael A. Stackpole
41. *Falcon Rising* (Twilight of the Clans, Volume 8) by Robert Thurston
42. *Threads of Ambition* (The Capellan Solution, Book 1) by Loren L. Coleman
43. *The Killing Fields* (The Capellan Solution, Book 2) by Loren L. Coleman
44. *Dagger Point* by Thomas S. Gressman
45. *Ghost of Winter* by Stephen Kenson
46. *Roar of Honor* by Blaine Lee Pardoe
47. *By Blood Betrayed* by Blaine Lee Pardoe and Mel Odom
48. *Illusions of Victory* by Loren L. Coleman
49. *Flashpoint* by Loren L. Coleman
50. *Measure of a Hero* by Blaine Lee Pardoe
51. *Path of Glory* by Randall N. Bills
52. *Test of Vengeance* by Bryan Nystul
53. *Patriots and Tyrants* by Loren L. Coleman
54. *Call of Duty* by Blaine Lee Pardoe
55. *Initiation to War* by Robert N. Charrette
56. *The Dying Time* by Thomas S. Gressman
57. *Storms of Fate* by Loren L. Coleman
58. *Imminent Crisis* by Randall N. Bills
59. *Operation Audacity* by Blaine Lee Pardoe
60. *Endgame* by Loren L. Coleman
61. *A Bonfire of Worlds* by Steven Mohan, Jr.
62. *Isle of the Blessed* by Steven Mohan, Jr.
63. *Embers of War* by Jason Schmetzer
64. *Betrayal of Ideals* by Blaine Lee Pardoe
65. *Forever Faithful* by Blaine Lee Pardoe
66. *Kell Hounds Ascendant* by Michael A. Stackpole
67. *Redemption Rift* by Jason Schmetzer
68. *Grey Watch Protocol* (*Book One of the Highlander Covenant*) by Michael J. Ciaravella
69. *Rock of the Republic* by Blaine Lee Pardoe
70. *Honor's Gauntlet* by Bryan Young

YOUNG ADULT NOVELS
1. *The Nellus Academy Incident* by Jennifer Brozek
2. *Iron Dawn* (*Rogue Academy, Book 1*) by Jennifer Brozek
3. *Ghost Hour* (*Rogue Academy, Book 2*) by Jennifer Brozek

OMNIBUSES
1. *The Gray Death Legion Trilogy* by William H. Keith, Jr.

NOVELLAS/SHORT STORIES

1. *Lion's Roar* by Steven Mohan, Jr.
2. *Sniper* by Jason Schmetzer
3. *Eclipse* by Jason Schmetzer
4. *Hector* by Jason Schmetzer
5. *The Frost Advances (Operation Ice Storm, Part 1)* by Jason Schmetzer
6. *The Winds of Spring (Operation Ice Storm, Part 2)* by Jason Schmetzer
7. *Instrument of Destruction (Ghost Bear's Lament, Part 1)* by Steven Mohan, Jr.
8. *The Fading Call of Glory (Ghost Bear's Lament, Part 2)* by Steven Mohan, Jr.
9. *Vengeance* by Jason Schmetzer
10. *A Splinter of Hope* by Philip A. Lee
11. *The Anvil* by Blaine Lee Pardoe
12. *A Splinter of Hope/The Anvil* (omnibus)
13. *Not the Way the Smart Money Bets (Kell Hounds Ascendant #1)* by Michael A. Stackpole
14. *A Tiny Spot of Rebellion (Kell Hounds Ascendant #2)* by Michael A. Stackpole
15. *A Clever Bit of Fiction (Kell Hounds Ascendant #3)* by Michael A. Stackpole
16. *Break-Away (Proliferation Cycle #1)* by Ilsa J. Bick
17. *Prometheus Unbound (Proliferation Cycle #2)* by Herbert A. Beas II
18. *Nothing Ventured (Proliferation Cycle #3)* by Christoffer Trossen
19. *Fall Down Seven Times, Get Up Eight (Proliferation Cycle #4)* by Randall N. Bills
20. *A Dish Served Cold (Proliferation Cycle #5)* by Chris Hartford and Jason M. Hardy
21. *The Spider Dances (Proliferation Cycle #6)* by Jason Schmetzer
22. *Shell Games* by Jason Schmetzer
23. *Divided We Fall* by Blaine Lee Pardoe
24. *The Hunt for Jardine (Forgotten Worlds, Part One)* by Herbert A. Beas II
25. *Finding Jardine (Forgotten Worlds, Part Two)* by Herbert A. Beas II

ANTHOLOGIES

1. *The Corps (BattleCorps Anthology, Volume 1)* edited by Loren. L. Coleman
2. *First Strike (BattleCorps Anthology, Volume 2)* edited by Loren L. Coleman
3. *Weapons Free (BattleCorps Anthology, Volume 3)* edited by Jason Schmetzer
4. *Onslaught: Tales from the Clan Invasion* edited by Jason Schmetzer
5. *Edge of the Storm* by Jason Schmetzer
6. *Fire for Effect (BattleCorps Anthology, Volume 4)* edited by Jason Schmetzer
7. *Chaos Born (Chaos Irregulars, Book 1)* by Kevin Killiany
8. *Chaos Formed (Chaos Irregulars, Book 2)* by Kevin Killiany
9. *Counterattack (BattleCorps Anthology, Volume 5)* edited by Jason Schmetzer
10. *Front Lines (BattleCorps Anthology Volume 6)* edited by Jason Schmetzer and Philip A. Lee
11. *Legacy* edited by John Helfers and Philip A. Lee
12. *Kill Zone (BattleCorps Anthology Volume 7)* edited by Philip A. Lee
13. *Gray Markets (A BattleCorps Anthology)*, edited by Jason Schmetzer and Philip A. Lee
14. *Slack Tide (A BattleCorps Anthology)*, edited by Jason Schmetzer and Philip A. Lee

MAGAZINES

1. *Shrapnel Issue #1*
1. *Shrapnel Issue #2*

The march of technology across BattleTech's eras is relentless...

Made in the USA
Coppell, TX
13 October 2020